MARKED FOR DEATH

A GRAY GHOST NOVEL, BOOK 6

AMY MCKINLEY

ARROWSCOPE PRESS, LLC

Marked for Death

Copyright © 2020 Amy McKinley

(p) **ISBN-13**: 978-1-7339425-9-1

(e) **ISBN-13**: 978-1-7339425-8-4

Publisher: Arrowscope Press, LLC; www.arrowscopepress.com

Editing—Kate B., Line Editor, Kristina B., Proofreader, Red Adept Editing

Cover Design—T.E. Black Designs; www.teblackdesigns.com

Interior Formatting—Arrowscope Press, LLC; www.arrowscopepress.com

1

KEEGAN

Washington, DC
Five Years Ago

In the dim light of the hotel room, I trailed my hand along Kara's bare leg, her soft skin irresistible. The steady rise and fall of her chest indicated she was asleep, and I studied her stunning features in that unguarded moment.

I didn't regret what we'd done for most of the night. Our paths crossing in the small tavern after my meeting couldn't have meant anything, no matter how much I wished otherwise. Her thick black hair fanned out against the stark white of the pillowcase, and I fingered a strand as my thoughts drifted.

She'd been beautiful when we'd met as kids in a horrible, fucked-up situation. She'd had someone there for her, though—her father. I'd had no one, no protector. It didn't matter, though. I'd already planned when and how I would leave. I knew she would be fine. Her stay of execution had always been temporary, but mine had been a lifetime sentence, ending on the day of my planned escape.

The familiar fury that lived and breathed inside me stoked to a virtual blaze at the thought of my past. Kara's face came back into focus—not the one of our youth, but the one in the present.

I had to get away from her. I needed to think. Seeing Kara again brought back all the old feelings of hopelessness and desperation. I felt trapped, but I hid it all behind a wall of muscle, power, and rage. No one knew what I was truly capable of. Maybe Kara had a sense, but not even she had gotten a full glimpse of the monster within.

The guys—my teammates, whom I'd gotten to know when I was a teenager—didn't have the whole story. I never offered, and they never demanded it. They had their own demons, and for that I was grateful. I had planned to take my secrets to the grave, which was a possible scenario, or they would all come tumbling out. And if that were to be my fate, I would do everything in my power to keep them from detonating at my team's—my family's—doorstep.

Some of my history would see the light of day if we stepped into the hornet's nest. At some point, I would have to open the door and beckon the guys inside at least enough to keep them safe. That's all that mattered to me. I would die for them. And there was a possibility that would happen.

Keegan

Present Day

I LEANED against the rough bark of a tree, unable to shake

the sense that the truth would catch up to me. A life built on false pretenses had only one likely outcome: it would inevitably come crashing down. A blast of hot wind whipped from the south, far too reminiscent of the nightmare that'd followed me from sleep and left my eyes gritty and dry as if I'd been in the actual desert instead of a comfortable bed in Maine.

Such omens demanded attention.

Too hot to run with a shirt on, I used it to wipe the sweat from my brow. It was early yet, and the day promised to be scorching. August often was, even in the back of Liam's yard, overlooking the cliffs in Maine. Whitecaps rolled, and the morning sun sparkled off the water's surface.

I hadn't committed to living there, as most of our team had. Instead, I bounced between Maine and California. Trev hadn't made the move yet—nor had Connor, Hayden, or Matt. It was only a matter of time until I put roots down in Maine, unless my past caught up with me. A part of me worried someone, one of my team or their wives, wouldn't want me here if it did, which is what held me back from relocating. I couldn't blame them.

The stakes were different now.

I shook my hair from my face. The longish mess was a necessity, one I'd decided on some time ago as part of my disguise. It was a far cry from what I used to look like, and I would keep it that way. I checked the time again then pushed off the tree to head to the scheduled meeting.

"Keegan, hold up!" Stella yelled from not too far behind.

I shut my eyes for a moment against what I knew was coming. She skidded to a halt.

"Oh God, what happened?" Her words were whispered, thickened with horror.

I felt the heat of her hand, centimeters from my back

before she pulled away. I turned and offered her a reassuring grin. "The scars are old. They happened in another lifetime." She was the only one of my teammates' wives who hadn't seen them. While I didn't want to have the conversation, at least it would be over with. I would put an end to it immediately. "Did you need something, Red?" I pulled my shirt over my head, concealing the map of scars on my back.

Stella tugged on a piece of her fiery hair, and the worry darkening her expressive eyes cleared. "Yeah, sorry. There's a call for you. Can you take it before the meeting? The guy's persistent and only wants to speak to you."

The day was already going from bad to worse. I felt it in my bones. I walked with her into the main house. She handed me the cell, and I took it upstairs to the room I was staying in so I could change and jot down any notes I needed. After shutting the door, I unmuted the call.

"Keegan here."

"Ah, good. Hello," the melodic cadence of a man's voice murmured. "Before we go any further, I must verify that you're the same person who knows Ankara."

My hand tightened on the phone, and I forced myself to relax before I cracked the device. "The city?"

"No."

It was a gamble. My pulse kicked up a notch as a memory of her long, dark hair sprawled across my pillow flashed through my mind. "Yes, I know her."

"I'm sorry, but I need confirmation before I tell you the reason for this call."

"I don't have time for this." *Games within games.* "Either say what you called for or stop wasting my time."

"It's important. I want to hire you to rescue someone, but I need to make sure you're the person she told me about."

She. It had to be her. Ankara was not her name, but it

was where her mother had come from and the nickname I used to call her when we were alone. A growl crawled up my throat, but I pushed it down. "Kara." That was all I was willing to say, no last names. *Is she in trouble?*

"Finally. I had a hard time tracking you down, as the name she gave was Max, but you matched the physical description. I'm Samir, and I'd like to hire you to rescue my four-year-old daughter." A slight tremor ran through his voice. "She isn't in danger yet, but it's coming."

I needed more information but didn't have the time. Plus, he'd said his daughter wasn't in immediate danger. I had to get to the conference room, so we set up an appointment to talk over Skype.

I disconnected and headed out, blocking the call from my mind—there would be time later to get lost in memories. It didn't take long to reach the meeting room, a large, warehouse-like structure between Liam's and Jack's properties. I pushed open the metal door and fell into a chair at the long table. Jack, Liam, Mike, Chris, and Hayden were waiting.

"Needed your beauty rest?" Hayden snickered at me just as Hawk slipped through the door behind me.

I returned Hayden's grin with a glare. "Just taking a page from your playbook." Everyone called Hayden pretty, and he didn't mind one bit. We looked alike, which was only a coincidence. His high cheekbones and brown hair that fell in loose curls almost to his shoulders mirrored mine. The physical difference between us was our eye color. Mine were hazel, more green than brown, and dripping venom regularly, or so I'd been told. Forged in hate, my demeanor was second nature.

Hayden was a happy-go-lucky kind of person who didn't take himself too seriously. Raised by his grams, he'd had a decent childhood for the most part. They'd been poor, and our school and surrounding neighborhood were not easy places to exist in without acquiring a fair share of bumps and bruises. Even so, his general good nature hadn't suffered. He'd grown on all of us from the first time we'd helped him out of a tight spot back in high school.

I'd lived several lifetimes of hell before I'd researched and joined the crew in California when I was sixteen.

"I've got Rich on the line," Mike announced.

Rich Stevens, our CIA contact, was someone for whom we performed rescue and recovery missions on occasion, among other jobs, through our company, Gray Ghost Security. Most of our team had known one another since our high school years.

"Good morning, gentlemen." Rich's deep voice sprang from the speaker and filled the room. "I received a call yesterday from a friend, George Hammond, who needs help. I suggested he utilize your team's skills. My hands are tied. The government will not intervene in ransom situations, and the police in Caracas have their hands full."

Caracas, Venezuela—where Kara lives. Dread sat heavily in my gut. The dream from last night reeked of premonition, of prophecy. I would be going back.

The country had been getting worse since I'd been there. There were dark zones, ruled by gangs and criminals, that the police avoided. The kidnap rate averaged five victims a day, regardless of the victims' wealth, and the police force there had an elite anti-kidnapping squad, but it seemed their plate was full.

"Why won't their police get involved?" Mike tapped a pen on the tabletop. "What do you know?"

"Not enough, unfortunately. We had a last-known location when one of the employees tried to call George. We know that the government seized George's company, GH Envirotech, some time ago, but the four American men who remained behind were extracting vital components to take home. They never made it."

"What vital components?" Jack asked.

"That hasn't been disclosed to us. George's partner, who ran the Venezuela branch, had a heart attack and passed away the day before the company was taken. Before his death, he'd messaged George some vague notes but not enough information to understand what they were working on. George is digging. As soon as I hear anything, you'll know."

"Have demands been made?" Mike asked.

"Yes. George was contacted, and the price is fifty thousand each for release."

Jack leaned forward. "Do we have proof of life?"

I crossed my arms over my chest and leaned back in the chair. It sounded like a quick mission, once we established where the kidnappers were holding them. The tension between my shoulders eased. I was worrying unnecessarily.

"Not visual, but we have audio from the phone call for ransom," Rich said.

"So we start with that." I wanted this mission—and the meeting—over. "Who's going?"

"A small team, three or four, should get the job done," Rich said.

Jack stood. "I'll go with Keegan and Hawk."

In and out, and hopefully, the past will stay where it belongs.

2

KEEGAN

I GAZED AROUND at our group gathered on the sandy Maine shores, and another notch of pain fell away. I would do whatever it took to keep them safe. I'd made the right choice all those years ago. They were my family, the one I'd wished for, the one I hadn't gotten from birth.

Laughter swelled throughout our small group. I tipped a water bottle to my lips and drank. The sun beat down, kissing the water in a starburst of sparkles, inviting us to cool off in the choppy water. I dropped into a chair and handed a bottle to Hawk, who sat with Stella to my right.

I drew another deep pull of the chilled liquid. It acted as a temporary antidote to the hot August day.

"Thanks." Hawk tapped the side of my drink with his, eliciting the sharp sound of crinkling plastic.

I angled the bottom of my water toward Stella. "May want some more sunscreen, Stel. You're burning." With her red hair and fair skin, she didn't do well in the sun for long.

She grimaced as she looked at her reddened skin. "I want to go into the water first, and then I'll get out of the sun." She stood and grabbed Hawk's hand. After he got to his feet, she turned to the rest of us. "Anyone else going in?"

"I am." Liv tucked her hand in Liam's and tugged at him. His mouth stretched into a wide grin, and he followed her willingly. Hannah, Jack's other half, wasn't with us for the next few weeks, as she was building a separate team of recruits for a newly sanctioned team.

Jack looked to his watch then shot both Hayden and me a serious look. "Our flight out is in a few hours. I'm heading up. We need to strategize some more."

I nodded. I would go, as well, after I enjoyed a few more minutes of happiness. I had a feeling the idyllic life I shared with my team would be threatened in some capacity and greedily soaked up every second I could before the storm hit.

Hawk and Stella returned half an hour later. Hayden was passed out, snoring softly. After an umbrella was set up and Stel curled in a chair in the shade, Hawk turned to me. "What's going on? I can feel the worry radiating off you."

A half grin curved my face. "We need to head up soon and go over the path we'll take to rescue the Americans. I'm going to take point on this one. It's a place I've been before."

Hawk's brows rose. "You don't talk about your life before we met."

There were many reasons why I hadn't. I would've been putting a target on Jack, Mike, and Hawk. They were fierce back then and had grown more so as we got older. But then, they were feral in their fight over what they had and what they believed in. It had fit with the caldron of emotions I'd kept buried. They were who I wanted to hang with. They fought for their lives and those they cared for with every-thing they had. To the death, if pushed far enough. I could relate. They'd accepted me into their core group after I'd joined in a few battles and they'd learned I had nowhere to live.

"I had no reason to then."

———

SHOWERED AND PACKED, Jack, Hawk, Chris, and I crowded around the conference table in our meeting room. Chris transferred the satellite feed onto the big screen along one wall, so we had a clear view of the hostages. He wasn't traveling with us but would monitor everything from afar. Something was going on with his brother, Trev, and he wanted to work both missions.

"Hawk mentioned you're taking the lead on this rodeo." Jack slid the laser pointer across the table.

I slapped my hand down before it rolled off the table. "Yeah. I know the area, although a lot has changed. The country is run as a dictatorship, even though they haven't officially announced the change in policy."

"We won't be welcome." Hawk's gaze scanned the image on the screen.

"No." He had no idea how true that statement was. "The jet will drop us here." I highlighted Aruba with the laser pointer. "Then we'll enter Venezuela under cover of night, on a boat. Trust is not something the people of Caracas give freely. But the country is starving, and their trust can be bought."

"So we'll go in with a large sum of cash," Jack inserted.

"Yes. And supplies. Food and the gel packs or gummies we use to hydrate when carrying a large amount of water isn't an option." I traced the path of entry, camouflaged by forest. "This is a way off from where we want to be, but it's well hidden and a good spot to stash the boat."

"Rich will have to get a US Embassy representative we can trust to leave a vehicle there for our use. Someone who will keep this information to himself and leave no paper trail." Jack jotted notes for what we would need as we planned.

"Civilian clothes, then." Hawk continued to scan the map.

"Yes. We'll have to blend well. Moving at night, despite how dangerous the city is, will be our best option." I highlighted an area where there was an inn no longer in business. "Have the official reach out to these people to get us a room. The place is deserted, and it should offer us the cover and location we need. Most of the people are not supporters of the Venezuelan president, as he has starved them and destroyed their businesses."

"We should be able to get in and out. Why the room?" Hawk asked.

"That's the plan, but there... things rarely go that way. It's our contingency should we need to lay low." I traced the path from the hotel a few miles away to where we had a visual of the crew that had our targets. "There are a lot of men here, and the fees they're asking for hostage release are high. In this country, they've had express kidnapping, where they negotiate with the hostages to get what they can from their families for release. But the large amount of money they're demanding indicates more of a criminal presence than the typical express kidnapping."

"So, you propose to enter here?" Jack circled the alley between two buildings.

"Yes. All of us on foot and hopefully with minimal gunfire."

The kidnappers appeared on satellite pictures as if there was no worry of a rescue by the way their backs were mostly to the cluster of four hostages bound on the ground and near the outskirt of the courtyard where they congregated. The machine guns many wore were a concern.

"That's the plan, then." Jack gathered the photos and stuffed them into an envelope. "I'll get the boat, vehicle, and room secured for us. Anything we need to know about your time there?"

"No. I'd prefer the past remain where it is."

"Should that change..." Jack waited.

"I'll bring you all up to speed if it does." *Hopefully never.* "If everything goes the way we've planned, this will be an in-and-out job with the government never knowing we were there."

The government wasn't the threat. It was the Dark Wings.

3

―――――

KEEGAN

UNEASE ITCHED under my skin as soon as we set foot in Venezuela. We illegally entered the streets of Caracas under the blanket of night. The government never would have allowed us entrance. The atmosphere reeked of danger. It should. In this politically torn country, gangs and criminals ran the streets after dark. People were starving, scared, and quickly losing hope.

We'll be in and out. I held that thought close to keep at bay the overwhelming urge to turn around and flee. Jack and Hawk were behind me as I guided us toward the last known location of the hostages. We tracked them from their first call then kept the satellite pointed on where they'd retreated. A general location lock was enough. We would find them.

A lot of time had passed since I was last there, but the streets were eerily familiar. The look of them had changed, but the sinister taste remained. Only this time, I was entering voluntarily, not escaping.

Due to the mission, we'd refrained from wearing standard military clothes. Instead, we had on jeans and long-sleeved black Henley shirts, despite the warm climate, with our gear strapped on or in backpacks. Blending as much as possible was necessary.

I signaled behind me that the building ahead was our goal. Voices and music floated from the courtyard behind the small structure in front of us. We crept forward as one. The crackle of a fire and sound of men laughing and cheering covered our approach. At the edge of the building, I got a good look.

The four male hostages were tied in two groups. Both were near the other side of the building, and their belongings, which we were also tasked to retrieve, were close to a metal garbage can that was on fire. Orange flames licked the air, casting a glow over the area. There were men with machine guns hanging at their sides and others with holstered weapons. Their attention centered on two comrades who arm-wrestled. A bet was in place, given the stack of money in the overseer's hand. For the time being, the Americans were not their focus.

I signaled for Jack and Hawk to approach from the opposite side. I would go around the left of the building. From behind, Jack squeezed my shoulder in acknowledgment.

When they were in position, I advanced. Light flickered the closer we came to the courtyard. Pressed against the brick wall, I waited. Around the corner and in the center of the building's open back area, the garbage-can fire provided light. There were seven men, not including the two sets of people tied back-to-back and sitting on the ground off to the left. There wasn't enough coverage. We had to go in strong. I pushed off the wall and raced toward the hostages, crouching low. The men didn't notice at first.

Jack and Hawk were sprinting from the other side. Efficiently and quietly, we snuck behind the three guards who'd inched closer to the revelry on the other end of the courtyard. Once in position, we focused on the hostages.

After a few more steps, we reached the men. "We're here to take you home," I whispered as my blade sliced through plastic ties and freed two of them. They slumped forward at the release. Jack and Hawk were at my side, and I shoved the hostages toward my teammates.

The Americans were in bad shape. Bruises and dried blood covered their faces. Hawk hoisted one man in a fireman's carry. Jack did the same with another. The last two rescued hostages stood on shaky legs. They turned at my indication to go toward my teammates. One of them scuffled along as quickly as he seemed capable. I would take the rear and provide cover. The bearded hostage didn't go far.

"Go," I commanded under my breath. I had to recover their gear. Noise rose at the other end of the courtyard. With beers in hand, the captors' conversation flowed. The other men had yet to notice us. We blended well and were trained to move like ghosts. In time, they would see us. The three guarding their charges would return any second.

The cry went up. Guns were drawn. Drinking had slowed down their reflexes, but it didn't matter. We'd been spotted. Three thugs advanced, the others slow to assess. I shoved the hostages closer to Jack and Hawk. One went. The other hesitated, wavering on his feet.

The bearded hostage took one step then another toward the pile of gear close to the men who'd begun to turn at their buddy's shout.

"Go." I grabbed the man I'd freed and gave him another gentle shove toward Jack and Hawk. I would provide cover. The other three men were with my team. Jack turned. I shook my head. I would handle it. The hostages were my priority.

My mind emptied of all but the three thugs. The biggest rushed toward me with his fist cocked back, arcing to slam into my head. I shifted, using his momentum, and shoved him away. Off-balance, he stumbled around me, and I bent to avoid the next guy, whose punch was already aimed at my chin. I gave a kick to his knee and heard a satisfying crack. He screamed and went down. More men turned. *Not good.*

The odds were not in my favor. With a glance behind, I was relieved to see that Jack and Hawk had gotten the others away. The bearded one must finally have gone with them. I didn't see him.

Not quite the extraction we'd planned, but it was close enough. Adrenaline fueled my every move. We would be out of there soon.

There was no longer a need for stealth. Gun in hand, I fired off a succession of shots, taking out the men with machine guns closest to me. There was a flash of silver, and two more went down, but not by my hand. Short gurgling sounded from the men, who each had a knife protruding from his throat. Then they were silent. A pool of blood spread on the ground.

I whirled around in the direction of the knives as a sleek woman decked out in black and wearing a high ponytail approached, her face covered with a ski mask. A man three times her width attacked. I fought off my own, stealing glances as I was able. The way she moved as she engaged in combat—I knew her. *Kara. What the hell is she doing here?*

I faltered from the shock of her presence. It cost me. I felt the burn of a bullet as it grazed the outer shell of my ear. The smooth exit my team had planned went up in smoke.

My guy was lying on the ground, and I swept up the

backpack we were told to retrieve. As I turned, a hard kick landed in my gut. Guns were going off. I had to keep moving. Kara blocked me. I dodged her feet. Then her fists came at me at a speed faster than they had when we were young.

Goddammit. A hard body slammed into me, and I turned to take out the guy who'd jumped me as her hands slipped beneath the strap and yanked. I struck back at her. The pack went flying. Another engaged with her, and we were momentarily busy, trying to take out our guys to get to the bag first. Seconds went by. She finished first.

"Where is it?" she yelled.

The guy went down. More approached, and I shot her a look. We were outnumbered.

Determination shone in her amber eyes. "Where's the bag?"

I scanned the area and caught sight of that stubborn hostage rounding a corner with the backpack over his shoulder. There was a swarm of criminals between him and us. With no choice, I grabbed her hand and yanked her with me as I ran.

Kara being sent to retrieve the bag as well meant there was more going on than we were led to believe. We needed to find out what. Quickly.

4

———

KARA

IT'S REALLY HIM. My gaze devoured him as he fought with grace and deadly precision. It wasn't how I wanted us to meet again, but it didn't matter—I had a mission and had to see it through.

Bullets peppered the air. Our gazes collided, and for a split second, we were a team again. Keegan snaked an arm around my waist, yanking my body against his. We crouched and sprinted for cover while he shielded me. Annoyance sizzled, mixing with the adrenaline pumping through my body. I didn't need him to take care of me. I pried his fingers off me as we ran. He was too distracting, and I couldn't lose focus. Too much was at stake, as it always was.

We cut across a parking lot as more men took notice of the disturbance. Keegan whirled and fired. We darted behind another building. I glanced over my shoulder. Two men rounded the corner. Dozens would soon follow. We needed a diversion.

A bullet whizzed by, too close. The burn of its nearness singed my arm. Keegan maintained pace beside me. I caught a glimpse of a dilapidated side door on the building to our left. Keegan must have, as well, because he tugged my arm. His shoulder crashed into the warped wood. It popped open. I followed. We wove through rows of desks in the dark office, looking for a way out. They would be on us any second.

The door banged against the opposite wall. They were inside. We were almost across the large room. I dipped my hand into a pocket on my vest and pulled out a grenade. Keegan pressed his mouth into a tight line just as I pulled the pin and tossed it. We dove for cover, and the weight of his body settled over mine. The grenade exploded, and debris rained down. Keegan's scent washed over me before the acrid smell of smoke filled my nose.

Intense gaze. Strong fingers. I swirled with dizziness at his touch. Then his deep, gravelly voice penetrated the ringing in my ears. "You okay?" he asked.

"Yes."

Keegan rolled to the side, and the pang of loss swept through me. *We weren't meant to be.* I shoved the longing away and pushed off the ground. We wove around the debris before he opened a window and we slipped through. He dropped down first then helped me.

My eyes narrowed as I considered what his angle might be. "You know, I'm capable of taking care of myself, right?" I whisper-yelled at him.

He grinned. "I do, but this gives me a reason to touch you."

I shivered despite the warmth of the night. We'd joined forces, in a way, and he fought admirably. Then again, he'd had those skills when we were younger. He saw to the heart of the matter and did what was necessary. Killing me didn't seem to be his objective. "I attacked you. What gives you the idea I want your hands on me?"

He ignored me as we ducked into another building. We maneuvered to a corner section, where each of us peeked through the windows. Men with machine guns crawled through the streets and alleyways. There were more than even he and I could take on. We were stuck.

From our vantage point, we had a view out the large storefront window. We could make out movement on the street, but they wouldn't be able to see us huddled there. It gave us a semblance of safety as we hid in plain sight.

The hairs on the back of my neck rose, and I turned to find Keegan scrutinizing me with his typical intensity. A pale shaft of light highlighted the green in his hazel eyes. Danger and power clung to him, the things that had drawn me when we'd first met. I'd felt safer with him around. The others had made me nervous, uncomfortable, and afraid. If I let myself dwell too long on the past, the old hurt rose from when he'd left.

"What's your objective?" Keegan growled.

"Probably same as yours," I replied evasively.

"Rescuing hostages? Why would the Dark Wings be interested in these Americans?"

"Not all of them. One in particular." I debated keeping the real reason to myself, but I didn't care enough about the task I was to complete to keep it a secret. "More so the backpack, which I was to secure at all costs, even above the man."

"What was in it?"

I didn't know and shrugged as an answer.

"Who ordered you to get it?"

"Does it really matter? I had a job to do. You of all people know what that's like. Very few questions are tolerated, if any."

Several seconds passed, and I had to remind myself to

breathe. He was like a live wire, and energy crackled between us—it always had. Being around him was like facing a panther that could strike at any moment. He was a predator. When he spoke, the tension eased slightly between my shoulder blades. We had time to kill while we waited for the thugs to move on and the manhunt to thin out.

His gaze crawled over my face before it dipped lower. "We didn't get much talking in last time we saw each other."

Heat infused my cheeks. Images burst in my mind from that night nearly five years before. The feel of him... what he did to me. I would never forget the pleasure. It was a once-in-a-lifetime kind of moment, something I cherished and knew I would never have again.

I chose my words with care. "I'm married."

A muscle ticked along his jaw. The sight of it sent a thrill through me. "How long?"

"Five years."

His brows rose. "You married shortly after? Were you engaged then?"

How to answer this one... "Not exactly. Soon after."

"Are you happy, Ankara?"

His voice had softened, and my heart fluttered at the nickname he'd given me and whispered in the dark of night. "Yes." I was, in a way. Samir was my best friend. What more could a girl want? *Keegan,* my traitorous heart screamed, but we weren't meant to be.

"And your father? I bet this makes Ahmed happy, although I'm not sure why you're still working with the Dark Wings. Unless this is something else?"

"I just do as I'm told." There was no way he could know. If he did...

Again, his penetrating stare bored into me, as if he could

see my very soul. Sometimes, I thought he could. But then he would know, so I must have been successful at shielding him from my deepest secrets.

"Are you in trouble?"

"No." I needed him to stop asking questions. "That night, when we were together—"

His features hardened. "It was one night. That's all it was."

I tensed, his words a slap to my already heated face. I was wrong—I was the one with the feelings toward him, not the other way around. "Right. Obviously, I've moved on." I hadn't, but I did have responsibilities. I let the silence stretch between us until I couldn't stand it any longer. We had history, and I let myself soften toward him a little. I reached out and ran my finger across the white ridge of a scar that curled over his shoulder and peeked through a tear in his shirt. Memories punched me in the gut. I'd caused that one and so many more. "I'm sorry." I swallowed back the guilt as I lifted my somber gaze to meet his.

A wall fell over his face, and I mourned the loss. He'd shut me out from his emotions. I wished I'd been the one to slip past his defenses, but I didn't think he'd ever truly let anyone in.

"They're just scars, Kara. They don't define or rule me."

A tremor raced through me as the images of how he got them flashed through my mind.

With the pad of his finger, he traced circles along my palm. "It wasn't your fault."

But it was.

5

―――――

KEEGAN

My bag thumped against the wall of the tiny hotel room. Hours before, the threat outside the building Kara and I were taking shelter in had calmed enough for us to go our separate ways. I couldn't go home with Jack and Hawk and had quickly communicated to them what had happened, that I was okay, and that I would be staying to search for the remaining American. After my check-in, they'd had to leave with the other three hostages, who weren't in the best of shape. They would be back.

Kara consumed my thoughts, and my mind traveled back to when we'd first met.

"I don't want to be here," she'd whispered just loudly enough for me to hear.

My heart hardened as I stared at the girl I was supposed to train. My hands were tied. I couldn't help her if she needed it. Sweat rolled freely down my back as we baked under the sun. She was tiny with a mass of long, black hair, maybe a year younger than my fifteen years. Pretty. "Then why are you here?"

She shrugged her bony shoulders, her whiskey-colored

eyes huge in her face. "We were paying respect to my mother's family in Ankara, and then... My father says I have to learn to fight. In case..."

So her mother was Turkish. My mind nagged me. *Who is her father? In case what?* An air of wealth surrounded her—she wore stylish clothes and carried herself in a way that suggested education. *Could she mean in case of an attack on her life?*

With my peripheral vision, I studied the tall, dark-haired man talking with Jamal, who ran the mercenary group. I took in the way her father stood and how his attention rarely strayed to those of us in training. He carried himself with an aura of importance. I couldn't get a read on the type of person he was, but it didn't matter. I was to train his daughter to defend herself and fight back.

Our band of mercenaries traveled between Jamal's base camps. There was one there, one near Caracas, Venezuela—where we would go in a few months, and a third that I didn't remember much of. That's where I'd started. It was in a desert, brutally, scorching hot. I'd lost time there.

My stomach growled. I ignored it. Nothing would come of breaking from training. There were four more boys close to my age, only a few years older, there. They barely kept us fed, except for when we completed the tasks required. Then, there would be a feast. My abs tightened, and I willed the weakness away.

The waif of a girl held her defensive position, as I'd instructed. I focused on that, not what or who her father was or my never-ending hunger. I doubted her father would be any help to me. The faster I got her up to speed, the better. I'd had plans, and they hadn't concerned her.

Three times, fate had brought us together. It wasn't a coincidence. With a concentrated effort, I let go of the past and focused on my other objective for Samir in Venezuela. I needed more information and would get it that morning. I pulled out the small tablet I'd brought on the off chance that something went wrong during our mission to rescue the American hostages. It had, but seeing Kara again was almost worth the botched job.

I powered up the tablet and checked the time. The Skype ping sounded at exactly 0900. I accepted the video call, and Samir's face filled the screen. He looked to be of Venezuelan descent with his brown skin, short, dark hair, and kind brownish-green eyes. After we exchanged greetings, we got down to the business he wanted to hire me for.

I directed the conversation where I needed it to go. "Who is it you want me to rescue?"

The strained smile on Samir's face fell. "My daughter."

"Is she with her mother?" I'd had Chris do a background check on him, but I hadn't had a spare moment to read it yet. I would. Nothing would happen until I got all the information.

"She is. Mostly." He ran a hand over his face. "We have a nanny who helps out when my wife is away on... business."

That sounded cagey. "I won't agree to take this job unless I know everything." And I wouldn't take the kid from the mother unless there was a damn good reason.

Samir scrubbed his face with his hands. I couldn't make out much in the background other than it looked like he was sitting in an office. A knock sounded, and his gaze darted up then softened. He clipped out a response. A half smile curved his lips, directed at whomever had entered, before he returned his attention to me.

"My wife is Kara, and from my understanding, you two have history." He paused, maybe in hopes that I would respond. "A lot is going on, but the most pressing concern is our daughter. I'm afraid she will be caught in the middle of what's happening around her."

Kara has a kid? A daughter. I sucked in a deep breath and forced my heart to return to a steady beat. Out of all the women I'd been with, she was the only one who'd infiltrated my worthless heart. "Why would you want your daughter taken from Kara?"

"Not taken from her." Samir's shoulders slumped. "I was on a business trip and called Kara to check in before my flight home. I could hear men's voices in the background. She was whispering and told me not to return, that it was too dangerous."

"Too dangerous for who?"

"Me. Kara is privy to information that I'm not regarding her father's dealings. While I know Kara can take care of herself, I worry our daughter will get caught in the crossfire."

"What exactly did Kara tell you to make you stay away?" *From your daughter.* The accusation shouted inside my mind. Anger burned hotly beneath the blank stare I'd perfected over the years.

Samir's brows furrowed. "The call cut off or she hung up, so I'm not sure. I check in and talk to my daughter every night, but Kara isn't always there. I think she worries the line is bugged."

"Wouldn't you know if Kara was safe? Or your daughter?"

He leveled a stare at me. "Not necessarily. My daughter should be—there is the nanny, Andrea, if Kara isn't by her side. There is a lot about my wife I understand and respect, including her short stay in the training camp during her youth."

Interesting. I wonder exactly how much she shared. "I won't get involved unless Kara is on board."

"I understand."

"I'll need verification from Kara personally. Is there anyone we can or can't trust in the household?" I knew where the house was, so there was no need to confirm. Lucky for me, I was already in Caracas.

"We trust Andrea, but that's it. There is one other thing." Samir looked to the side of the screen.

Someone else was in the room with him, listening. "Who else knows about this?"

He pursed his lips, and a moment passed. "My business associate, David Meyer. I'm here with him in Washington, DC."

"David Meyer of Meyer Ancestry Labs?" I'd heard of them. They specialized in collecting genetic data. If anything, it was information to file away in case it was important later.

"Kara knows where I am. But her warning not to come home has me very concerned. There are things... Her father, Ahmed, is up to something." He cleared his throat. "I'll get word to Kara and have her contact you. Then will you agree to help?"

"Most likely, so long as I have confirmation from Kara about extracting the child."

"I'll make sure she finds time to speak with you."

"What can you tell me about Ahmed?"

"I know very little about Kara's father's business dealings, other than the ones we are involved in together. Those are more of an investment for him than anything else, and I don't see how that's where the threat is coming from. The gray area is when Ahmed involves Kara. Usually, I'm kept in the dark. This time, she was anxious."

"Worried about what? Which business deal?"

"That's the thing. I don't have anything coming up that involves Ahmed, so I'm unsure, and she couldn't say. Just that it wasn't safe for me specifically to come back."

We disconnected the call with an understanding that Samir would get the confirmation from Kara that I needed. If I'd known they were married, I would have asked her myself last night. I wondered why she hadn't brought it up. I leaned back against the chair. *What the hell is going on?*

I couldn't even begin to wrap my head around Kara having a kid. Part of me was angry with her, with Samir. He had the only woman I'd ever wanted. *They're a family.* I rubbed absently at the ache in my chest.

Kara's attack was mission-based. I knew not to take it seriously. Contact with her outside of that one-off would be digging a deeper hole and would open the door to the past and invite my team in. I dreaded the remote possibility of that happening.

I couldn't do it. I couldn't tell them who I was or where I came from. I didn't want to risk losing the guys who'd become my family. Maybe I wouldn't have to share everything. I would fill them in on what they needed to know to keep them safe, so that they would have a grasp of the mission I would embark upon alongside the original rescue and recovery.

Something about the timing of Samir contacting me along with the hostage mission nagged me, and I wondered if they were intertwined.

I typed a few things on the tablet, searching for information about Kara and Samir's wedding. Their presence on the internet was very small, but I got what I wanted.

My finger hovered over the button to connect me with my team. There were a few things I had to share with them.

Drumming my fingers on the desk, I ran through how much to tell them, discarding the majority of my past, which shouldn't have been necessary. With a few taps on the keyboard, I had Jack on the screen.

"Did you locate him?" Jack referred to the missing hostage.

"No, not yet. But I have another development that may be related."

Hawk moved into the screen's field too. Good—I would need both of them. I ran my hands through my hair and tugged on the too-long strands before spilling part of my connection with Kara. "Remember that call I took before our meeting with Rich?"

"The one Stella answered?" Hawk leaned forward, his blue-gray eyes bright against the contrast of his brown skin.

"Yeah, that one. I had another meeting with the guy a few minutes ago, and I took the job."

"We need to finish this one first," Jack interrupted.

"I think the two may be connected."

"How so?" Jack's eyes narrowed.

"The guy's name is Samir Medina, and he wants me to extract his young daughter from Venezuela and a potentially dangerous household. Before you ask, there's more. The house is owned by Ahmed Hernandez, who is a political advisor to the Venezuelan president. Ahmed's daughter, Kara, and her husband live in the same household as the ambassador."

"How does this relate to the hostage that's gone missing?"

"Kara is the woman who ambushed the rescue. She was after the same man, or more specifically, what he had on him."

"Who is she working for?" Jack's gaze narrowed further.

"Not positive." Acid churned in my gut. "Possibly her father."

"How exactly do you know her?" Hawk, normally quiet, zeroed in on the root of the problem.

"Remember that job we did in Afghanistan?" At their nods, I spilled the only part I wanted to share about how Kara and I were acquainted. A flash of long black hair, soft skin, and full lips hijacked my mind until I ruthlessly shoved the images away. "It was right after that when we'd gone to DC to debrief. I ran into Kara in a bar, and we spent the night together."

Jack tapped a pen against the desk. "How does the husband know about you? Could this be a setup? Was she married at the time?"

"No, it's not, and she wasn't married then." I'd done my research after talking to him. "Shortly after, though. About three months, to be exact."

"We don't take kids from their parents unless there is a damn good reason."

One like our upbringing. Jack hadn't said it, but by the somberness that fell around us, we were all thinking about it.

"I told Samir that too. He'll find a way to speak to Kara or record the call so I get confirmation. I know her voice." Damn well.

"This still doesn't explain why things are bad in her household. Or why Kara was after our hostage. Who is this woman?" Jack shot Hawk a look before facing the camera once more. "Makes me wonder what the American had from George Hammond's company."

I ignored Jack's question about Kara. I couldn't go there with him.

"We'll push back on Rich to learn more," he said. "You see what you can find out from Samir."

"The hostage may have been recovered, just not by us." Hawk aired my concern.

"If I can get Kara and her daughter out of there, I have a feeling we'll learn a hell of a lot more."

Jack nodded. "Agree. Hawk and I will be leaving tonight. We'll reconvene at"—he checked his watch—"oh five hundred."

I closed down my tablet and stowed it in my pack. *What are you involved in, Kara?*

6

KEEGAN

Hᴏᴛ, bitter coffee slid down my throat as I mentally went over the details of our botched rescue mission almost two days ago. Dawn was fast approaching, and in my tiny hotel room, there was little noise from the city street below. With the sunrise, the criminals were mostly back in their holes.

My hand gripped my 9mm at the slight sound of the doorknob turning. I pointed to where the intruder would enter. Jack and Hawk were due to return any second. It should be them, but I would never assume. I'd learned that lesson long ago.

Through the gun's sight, my gaze trained on the door. It swung open, and Jack and Hawk stood there, guns raised and smirks curving their mouths.

"You guys are idiots." I lowered my gun and gave up fighting the grin tugging at my lips. Hawk shut the door behind him, and I set my weapon on the table.

Jack eyed my drink. "Got any more of that?"

I nodded to the small carafe I'd made in anticipation of their arrival. We had to strategize. After getting coffee, they sat at the chipped, round table with me.

"How are the men you pulled out?" I needed some good news to offset the shit-show of a mission.

"Battered and dehydrated, but they'll recover quickly," Jack answered. "About the missing guy, Henry Adams... We don't have a visual anywhere, but since Kara is also hunting him, trailing her would be a good place to begin."

"We'll start at her father's home." I finished the last of my coffee then stood to gear up. It'd be better to head out before the sun was high in the sky.

My phone vibrated from a text. Jack's and Hawk's must have, too, as they were looking at their screens. I tapped in the code to unlock my cell and reveal a group text from Chris. An encrypted email was found on George Hammond's server, from the former partner of GH Envirotech's Caracas branch to his partner, George, in the States. Chris said he should have the encryption broken within the hour and would continue to search for others. I bet good old George was holding out on us. That pack the missing American had contained something he didn't want anyone to know about.

"Hopefully, we'll learn what's in the bag Henry had." Hawk said what we were all thinking.

"We're supposed to hang tight until Chris gets the information from the email," Jack said.

I was itching to get out there for another glimpse of Kara, even though it was dangerous. Seeing her again had been like imagining a forbidden but desperately desired drink of water while stranded in the desert. I would have given everything to consume that water.

Ambient light spilled through the window as the sun inched higher, and the pressure of our mission, the need for action, increased with each passing minute. The streets were no longer silent and eerie with anticipated malice, as people woke and went about their days.

Jack crossed his arms over his chest, and a speculative gleam lit his hazel eyes.

I prepared for the inquisition that I knew was coming.

"So this woman, the one who attacked you during the rescue, who does she work for?"

I didn't want to get into it, but I could evade for the time being. It was safer for them if I did. "I already told you who her father is. She probably works for him. Whatever is in that backpack that Henry was so desperate to retrieve must be big. My guess is that's why Kara was sent to recover it. There must be a political connection to the contents. And her father is one of the advisors to the Venezuelan president."

Jack appeared to mull over the summary, and I held my tongue. *I should tell them, but what good would it do?* What I needed over everything else was to get them out of there and away from the Dark Wings' reach.

The heavy weight of Hawk's gaze beckoned, and I skimmed his features. We had one thing in common, and I'd given it away that night he'd shared his darkest secrets with the team. By the way he watched me, I knew he remembered my reaction to his father's betrayal when he offered a trade—Hawk for the debt he owed to save his skin.

I shuttered my expression, effectively locking him out. There would be no good in sharing with them, not about the Dark Wings. I'd been forced to take a vow, and breaking it would bring detrimental consequences to my brothers. Hawk was the quiet one. He wouldn't call me out. Not now. It would take a lot for him to press me for information because he'd planned to take his history to the grave and probably would have if it wasn't for his past that had come knocking at our door. I hoped with everything in me that the same wouldn't happen to me.

"About Kara." Jack broke into my thoughts. "Why—"

The buzz from our phones stopped him and brought a short reprieve from further questioning. He wouldn't let the coincidences with Kara go. If I could get Kara and her daughter home, I would have a better shot at keeping everyone safe and separate from Kara, her father, and the Dark Wings.

"Chris got it." Jack scrubbed his face. "Drone prototypes. The company was making insect-sized surveillance drones for the US in a foreign country. The wording is vague. We aren't sure if there was anything else to the drones. Regardless, this changes everything."

That's what had to have been in the backpack that Henry Adams and Kara were both so intent on possessing.

Hawk tossed his cell on the table and stood. He made his way to the open window and the hot breeze that wafted through it. Noise from the street below carried to the second floor we were on. It was a busy area, useful to get lost in.

I skimmed the message and got the same details. It seemed that George Hammond wasn't honest in his quest to retrieve his four employees. The email was from Henry Adams, and we could assume he was the next in line behind George's partner, who had died. Henry wasn't all that innocent after all.

"It shouldn't be too hard to find Henry, with his facial scarring." Other than when he wore sunglasses, his drooping eyelid and burn marks were visible, covering the right side of his face. The scarring his beard didn't hide would be easy to spot.

Rich's name flashed on Jack's cell before he answered. Our CIA contact's viewpoint about not being able to get involved had to have changed after the intel Chris had uncovered. Finding and recovering the drones would take precedence over everything. My Skype app pinged. *Samir.*

I moved away from the guys so Samir wouldn't pick up any information he shouldn't before accepting the call.

Samir's face filled the screen. Behind him were stainless-steel appliances and modern white cabinets. If he was calling from wherever he was staying, it obviously was not a hotel.

"I'm so glad you picked up." His hair was mussed, and wrinkles covered the blue button-down dress shirt he wore. "I have a recording of my conversation with Kara. She spoke directly to you." He held up his phone then pressed Play.

Kara's voice came through clearly enough to understand. "M—Keegan. You owe me, and I'm cashing in."

I could hear the frustration in her tone. She'd almost called me by the name she'd known me by, the one that was long dead and buried. As for owing her, I could only think she meant when I'd left her behind. I shook the cobweb of memories away and listened intently to what she said.

"Come get Lily. The nanny will meet you at the southwest corner of the yard. She's all that matters."

Tension dripped from Kara's voice and hit me in the gut. She was in trouble—that much was clear, especially if she wanted her daughter far away. Chills raced along my arms, and I knew I would do anything to help her.

Samir set the phone on the counter in front of him while another man entered the screen, his hand falling on Samir's shoulder as he placed a cup of coffee at his elbow. *Who is that guy?* I filed away the details in my mind for later. Something about him was familiar. *Could that have been David Meyer?*

"Will you help?" Samir's voice centered me once more on what needed to be done.

"Yes," I answered. "Did she tell you when the nanny will be outside?"

He shook his head. "I'm sorry, I don't know. My guess would be late afternoon, but I'm hesitant to say for sure in case they're there this morning."

I wrapped up the call and rejoined Jack and Hawk, who were off the phone as well. "What are our orders?"

Hawk's mouth was pressed into a tight line.

Jack responded. "Recover the contents of the bag at all costs. Henry is no longer a priority, but we're to retrieve him regardless for questioning."

I filled them in on my call with Samir. "If we find Kara, chances are she'll know the whereabouts of either Henry or the drones."

"Looks like we're going to rendezvous with the nanny." Hawk slung his gear on his back.

We agreed with extracting her daughter, as Kara would ultimately lead us to our directive.

I couldn't wait any longer. "Let's go."

7

KEEGAN

HAWK CROSSED his arms over his chest then pushed back so that his chair balanced on its back legs. I'd almost had them out the door earlier, but Jack talked sense into me, and I agreed that we needed to see the satellite feed of Ahmed's property first.

He, Jack, and I were holed up in the hotel room, waiting, and I couldn't escape Hawk's piercing blue eyes. I could practically see the calculations happening in his mind. He wasn't going to let it go, not after he'd come around and spilled his darkest secrets that night in the cabin in California, with Stella bearing witness to his demons.

"We have a few minutes until the feed downloads." Jack pushed back from the table, stood, and stretched.

Hawk continued to study me, and I refused to turn away. Even though he was the quiet one of our group, I knew he would be the one to push for answers. I'd slipped up that night in California and let him see how enraged I was over what his dad had been willing to do to save his own skin.

"There's something else that connects you to this

woman, isn't there?" Hawk's deep voice halted our movements. "What aren't you telling us?"

Darkness unfurled as the past crowded my present reality. I didn't want to bring them in any deeper than I had to. "Kara and I knew each other in the past, but I don't want to go into specifics." I glanced at Jack, who studied me. When we were in high school, Jack never pushed me to tell him where I'd come from or what demons haunted me. I respected him for that. Hawk had been the same, until recently. Things changed for Hawk when his wife, Stella, came along.

I liked Stella. She didn't take herself too seriously and had a fierceness about her when it came to those she loved. We'd seen it firsthand with her screwed-up brother. At first, she was wary of me, if not downright afraid. That dissipated fast, and I counted myself lucky to be in the circle of those she cared about and would fight for with all she had.

Another few seconds of silence stretched between us, and then Jack seemed to come to a decision. "Bring us into the loop if it becomes something we need to know."

That response represented why he was and always had been our unofficial leader. A good portion of tension melted away as I nodded to him. Hawk dropped his little inquisition as well.

I wished there was another way to get Kara's daughter out and to locate the American, Henry Adams. Having Jack and Hawk with me exposed them to danger that I'd experienced firsthand. If we were lucky, we would only encounter Ahmed. The odds were not in our favor, and the less they knew, the safer they would be.

"The feed downloaded." Hawk drew our attention to the laptop.

We huddled around the satellite video that Chris was

able to get of Ahmed's house. It was a short clip, but we got useful information from it. Guards patrolled the vast property in fifteen-minute intervals. We would need to get past the chain-link-and- barbed-wire fence that surrounded the backyard. There was space between that and the natural border of foliage that obscured the gate from being seen from the home. It would also conceal us.

I zoomed in on the live satellite feed of the front of the estate. People were congregating, some with signs, some without. Outraged fists pumped in the air. The government wasn't looking out for its people, and they were angry. The nation was rich in resources, but the profits were not being shared with the impoverished public. If that wasn't bad enough, they severely lacked access to medical care. With Ahmed's obvious wealth and political position as one of the president's supporters and advisors, he was a daily target. For the moment, they were protesting but staying on the outside of the wrought-iron gate—that could come in handy as a needed distraction.

The property was large and well-manicured, and the house sprawling and stately. It wasn't hard for me to think of Kara growing up there. The home was unfamiliar, as I didn't have any memories of where Kara lived. That's not where we met. And her father... I knew him by sight, but that was it, though I picked up from afar that he was cold, authoritative, and dangerous.

From surveillance to gearing up, we were ready in no time. My mind was divided between the mission and the need to see Kara again. Chills danced over my skin despite my gear and the heat. I'd never been able to exorcise her from my thoughts.

Thirty minutes later, we had left the hotel. Jack and Hawk agreed with me that we would stake out the southeast side of the house all day if we had to. There was a good chance we'd learn something useful, and the faster we could get in place, the better.

We were mere feet from the fence we would have to scale. The barbed wire at the top didn't matter for us, and it wasn't visible past the natural border of shrubs and trees that lined the inside, separating security from the view of the backyard. But with the extraction of a child, going over the top was not ideal. Jack pulled wire cutters from his pack while Hawk and I took the post to watch for anyone who might see what we were doing.

From Chris's intel on Ahmed's home, we'd learned there weren't any cameras aside from one by the front door, which fit Ahmed's narcissistic personality. When we were young, Kara had filled me in a little about Ahmed—he was secure in his authority with the Dark Wings on his payroll. My guess was that even though there were protests, he wouldn't contemplate that anyone could breach his sanctuary.

With the sun high and a warm breeze rustling through the foliage, we eased into place. Jack and Hawk were staked out ten feet from me on either side. None of us was in view of another. If the nanny approached the southwest side of the lawn, we had it covered.

Nestled between two trees that acted as one of the lines of defense against any uninvited guests viewing Ahmed's property, I maintained cover. Bypassing the fence and evading the guards who walked the perimeter at timed intervals hadn't been an issue for the three of us. One of us would be able to secret away the nanny and Lily, should the opportunity arise.

Time ticked by slowly. We'd been there over an hour, the thick shrubbery shielding us well. Our distance from the front buffered the roar from the protesters, and the diversion helped to keep the majority of the guards stationed at the entrance.

Through the branches, I caught movement behind the windows in the sprawling three-story home. The fact that Ahmed had such blatant wealth while the country he supposedly championed suffered caused my muscles to tighten with barely suppressed hatred. There always had been something I didn't like about that man. I shifted to alleviate the need to scratch my neck where leaves brushed it.

The flash of long dark hair caught my attention, and my gut tightened. Kara moved just beyond the glass doors of the second-floor balcony. Another person entered the room, but I wasn't able to see clearly. The French doors swung open, and she walked out, resting her elbows on the railing, her gaze scanning the section where we waited. A slight shake of her head told me all I needed to know. Lily wouldn't be out yet.

The breeze stirred, sifting through her hair like invisible fingers. Mine itched to do the same, to feel the silkiness of her skin. The memory of our night together flooded my mind, and desire for her crashed over me like a wave.

Five years before, I'd caught sight of her through the tavern window as she walked the sidewalk near my hotel late at night. I was on my feet and outside before even thinking. The streetlamps highlighted the curve of her face, and before I'd known my intentions, I'd whispered her name—close enough for her to hear. One look was all it had taken for years to fall away.

We'd shared a drink at the bar then left and gone to my room. What happened between us played on repeat. I was distracted. She had that effect on me. Nothing good would come of not being on my game, especially with the possibility of my past and present colliding.

8

———

KEEGAN

THE MORNING TURNED to late afternoon as hours ticked by. When we'd first arrived, we'd dodged the guards and set up micro cameras in the trees so we could monitor the house. I'd had a feeling we would need them at some point.

We waited, camouflaged by the trees and shrubs. Jack was more than twenty feet to my left, and Hawk an equal distance to my right. We had the southeast side covered.

The protests at the front gate had increased, drawing more guards away from the back to maintain security. That too worked in our favor.

As I'd done what felt like a million times in the last few hours, I scanned Ahmed's house for movement behind the windows of the three-story brick-and-stucco home. The door to the ground-floor patio opened, and an older woman emerged with a small child in tow. As the door swung closed, someone caught it from inside and stopped it, following close on the heels of the pair.

The three of them were far enough away that I couldn't make out their features, but I would have known Kara anywhere. The way she moved her limbs, her long black hair that had blue highlights when the sun hit it just right, and the way her amber eyes would pierce my soul. She was tempting when we were young, and I had to fight to keep an emotional distance from her. As a woman, she was damn near irresistible.

Kara spoke to an attractive woman not terribly older than herself who had to have been the nanny. Without pointing, Kara looked at where we hid. *This is it.* The nanny, who was probably a good ten years older than Kara, took the little girl's hand and headed toward the area of the yard where we were stationed. I stopped myself from stepping out from the trees so they would know where to go. That would've been a terrible move. Guards patrolled the perimeter of the house itself, and someone would have seen me. Our plan for taking the young girl was through a snatch and grab. It sucked, but there wasn't any other way.

The nanny and the little girl, Lily, neared the edge of the south side of the yard. My gaze alternated between them and Kara, who had turned back to the door as it opened. Ahmed joined her, and they engaged in a heated discussion I couldn't hear. I divided my focus between the little girl and Kara. Her posture tensed. Kara and Ahmed were arguing. Ahmed stepped toward the nanny. Kara went to block him. He barked out an order to come back immediately.

Kara snapped at him, but I couldn't quite make out what she said.

Ahmed moved fast, his palm slicing through the air. He'd backhanded his daughter. I could hear the strike across Kara's face from here. Rage sizzled inside me. The little girl cried out and ran to her mom, wrapping her arms around Kara's legs.

With Kara's training, she could've retaliated, but she

didn't. I locked out the dark emotions that demanded retribution. *Get her daughter.* She would never forgive me if I rushed forward to defend her at the cost of her daughter's freedom. There was more at stake than I dared risk. I ground my teeth and held my position, but being around Kara compromised my focus.

She and I lived messed-up lives.

All four of them—Kara, Lily, the nanny, and Ahmed— stood in a small circle, arguing while five guards flooded into the yard. Kara herded the nanny as she untangled her daughter's arms from her legs, pointing them in the direction of the house.

Our small window of time slammed shut. I stepped farther into the hedge. Every muscle froze at the bite of steel at my throat and prick on my side, near my right kidney. My mind whirled. I hadn't heard anyone approach. Alarm spread as I considered who it could be.

"I hardly recognized you," a man growled.

Revulsion and the ingrained childhood fear shot through me in a toxic spill. "Hugo."

"That's right, boy." He chuckled. "The prodigal nephew returns. Just in time to pay me back for all I've done for you."

His voice sent me back to a place I fought to keep buried.

Battered by the sand, blazing sun, and an empty stomach. Past images assaulted me, shredding the man I'd become in a blinding display of despair.

That wasn't my life. It wasn't real, not anymore. But Hugo's presence brought it all back: the hopelessness, the abuse, the relentless training, and the soul-destroying missions. With determination, my vision cleared, and the opulence of Ahmed's home once again greeted me.

From our position, Jack and Hawk wouldn't know what

was happening. My comm was muted, the private conversation—and I hoped the only bloodshed—between the two of us only.

"How did you know I'd be here?" I needed more information and time for Jack and Hawk to get away. We'd planned our exit strategy, with or without the girl, in different directions that converged where we were bedding down.

"Fool girl gave you away."

Kara had been right about the tapped line. She'd risked too much by talking on that phone. "She didn't give me away."

"That's right. She didn't give us everything. We were watching, and when I spotted you, I volunteered. What kind of a name is Keegan? You never did have any respect, Max."

"Not for you." I needed him to make a mistake. One slip, and I could break free.

"You have a family obligation. It's time you fulfilled it."

Hugo pressed the knife against my side as he moved us forward. If he didn't have the other one at my carotid, I'd have taken him down and killed him.

"There'll be no more hiding, Max."

We inched past the berm's threshold, which had become visible. I locked eyes with Kara. She'd moved closer, and I could see the horror that bloomed across her features. The nanny and little girl were whisked inside by two of the guards. Ahmed crossed his arms, waiting even as the remaining three guards urged him to go in. He must have wanted to witness Hugo's kill. That wouldn't happen yet. Hugo had made it clear he wasn't done with me.

As the pressure on my kidney lessened, I reacted. I grabbed his wrist and twisted, pulling his blade from my neck, shoving his elbow into his side, then dislodging the weapon digging into mine. I pivoted to end him and got a good look at him.

Holy hell.

Scars. The drooping eye. The beard. Hugo was Henry Adams, the hostage we'd been hired to rescue.

My legs were swept out from behind me, and I landed hard on my back. I was too stunned by Kara's face to react.

I'd always known she would be my downfall.

Kara followed me to the ground in a lightning-fast move. Her hand wrapped around my throat. A knife pierced my chest. Black dotted over my vision as the pressure against my windpipe increased, and I went under.

The darkness parted. *Was I under long? Seconds?* I held still, assessing and fighting the urge to lunge up and attack. My mind screamed to hold still. I had to trust my instincts where Kara was concerned. If I gave in to the physical need to fight back, I could end up killing her.

I couldn't. Not her.

Warmth had spread along my left pectoral where her knife had gone in. It should have struck my heart, but it hadn't—she'd angled the blade. *She'd meant to injure me, not kill me. She's covering me.* I would wait. There had to be a reason.

The cut would bleed but wasn't dangerous—it was more of a surface wound. Sounds filtered my way, invading my mind's analytical catalog. I locked on to her voice.

"I'll send someone for cleanup. Go inside and check to make sure there isn't anyone who got in." She spoke in Spanish, but when we'd fought during the hostage rescue, she'd used English. It didn't matter which she language she used—we were both fluent in many.

"I have orders to remain out here," the guard protested.

Kara stepped closer. "I gave you an order. He was the only threat, and now he's dead. Go, or you'll draw your last breath. Send Ricardo to help me. He doesn't have a problem with orders."

There was no rebuttal. The swish of the grass told me the guard slunk away. Kara bent down as I opened my eyes. Lines bracketed her mouth, and her gaze darted to the shrubs. "Hugo tipped off Ahmed. You have to leave before Ricardo gets here."

I raised my eyebrows at her. "And when he does arrive?"

"I'll handle it. Don't worry." She glanced over her shoulder. "Ahmed will be informed that you're dead."

"Where did he go?" I had to work to suppress my anger about being stabbed. More than anything, I wanted his head.

"I don't know. I have to get inside. I'll be downtown tomorrow. Find me."

She shoved at my shoulder, and I rolled to the cover of the trees. When I was clear, I watched as she jogged back to the house. *Where the hell are the rest of the guards?* Everything had happened in a matter of minutes, with no real alarm raised. The entire thing was odd.

From my peripheral vision, I saw Jack and Hawk sprint to me as I cleared the shrubs. We didn't have long before the guards would circle our side of the yard. Jack's hand snaked around my bicep, and I let him pull me to my feet.

We had to get away before the guards arrived. Why they hadn't remained was a puzzle that I needed to solve. Past the brush, I shoved Jack and Hawk off me and motioned for us to leave. "I'm okay. Nothing major was hit."

"There's a lot of blood," Hawk snapped under his breath as we cleared the fence and broke into a sprint.

"It's a surface cut." I ignored how Jack's gaze jerked to mine for a split second. I was sure he was remembering what I'd done during an interrogation when we were searching for Stella, who had become Hawk's wife. There had been blood everywhere when I'd interrogated one of the men about Stella's abduction, which I'd done more as a scare tactic than anything else. But the guys hadn't known that at first and assumed I'd snapped. I hadn't. We were taught well, and Kara knew what she was doing when she stabbed me. When I realized the ruse, I'd played along with her. After all, there was a lot at stake.

"You need to tell us everything." Jack's no-nonsense tone caused a barrage of unwanted images of what I'd have to relive while I shared my truth with them to slip through my mind. It would be a long couple of hours, and I worried about how they would react. It could shake the foundation I'd built with the guys, the only family I'd known since my parents were killed.

We were close to our base of sorts, our room, when Jack's cell buzzed. He shot us a wary glance then answered. After a few short words, he disconnected. We continued to our destination. Once behind closed doors, he spoke.

"That was Rich. A National Assembly leader collapsed after a meeting with the Venezuelan president and his advisors. He was actively opposed to the president and the dismal state of the people. He'd planned to back anyone who ran against the president in the next election. They've determined the cause was a small puncture wound like the drones would have made. Our timeline has narrowed due to the upcoming US meetings about the president."

"When is that scheduled to take place?" Dread pooled in my gut. The drones and who possessed them were our new mission's top priority. If nothing else, at least we knew they were still here.

Jack ran a hand through his short hair. "We have seven days."

9

KEEGAN

Jack's call with Rich rolled around in my head along with our newly adjusted timeline and the conversation I was about to have with my team about Kara and my past. I hadn't even said anything, but I already felt exposed. There was no other way to describe how that one incident in Ahmed's perimeter had catapulted into the disaster that would ensue. My uncle knew where I was, the name I hid under, and that Kara was a weakness, and only death would follow.

I stayed still while Hawk cleaned, butterflied, and bandaged the cut on my chest. I wished the lie she told Ahmed would trickle to Hugo, masking the fact that I still lived.

Time felt warped, and at that moment, I was back in the desert, living a hell no kid should. Hugo's voice anchored me to the years I'd spent learning that death was a luxury I was not permitted.

A hot blast of air tumbled me back in time. My heart regulated to a slow, steady thump as I pressed against the back of a sand ledge, the natural overhang protecting me from sight. As hot as the desert was during the day, it was equally as cold at night. I only wore threadbare tan pants, better to blend into the stark surroundings.

Sand granules shifted beneath the camels' hooves. Still, I waited. A few feet away, the small party would pass in a matter of seconds. Then I would strike.

No one spoke. They passed, and I sprang into action. There were four of them. One target. All would die.

It was them or me.

I sucked in air, willing the past to stay where it belonged despite the looming battle with my uncle and most likely Jamal, who had been my jailer, in a sense.

I blinked rapidly and shook off the memory.

It hadn't taken long to return to the hotel room with Jack and Hawk. We gathered around the small table, and I forced myself to stay seated rather than pace the room like a caged tiger while I invited them into the world I came from.

Hawk was eerily still, which was in his nature and made him a hell of a good sniper. Banked energy rolled off Jack and amped up my aggression. The temperature had climbed to the mid-eighties and held. As we approached evening, the sun shone at an angle where light spilled through the window.

Sitting was a lost cause, so I got up and grabbed three waters. I limited my movements enough to give the butterfly bandages time to adhere properly. The wound barely registered. It was shallow. I'd had much worse. After tossing Jack and Hawk each a bottle, I downed half of mine. *No more stalling.* I paced to the window and back, compelling the words to leave my mouth.

"You know that hostage that got away during the rescue? Henry Adams? Well, he's really Hugo Chavez, my uncle, and he is not a good man. And he's got the backpack with the drones. It changes things... like how we go after him." My muscles tensed, wanting a fight, but there wasn't a target there for me to take my aggression out on.

"We'll have to let Rich in on some of this," Jack interjected.

God, no. "Only what we need to. I won't admit we're related or anything that ties to my past. This has to stay between us. The dynamics are going to become skewed." I didn't want to tell them everything, but they had to know how bad things would get.

"We'll figure it out," Jack said.

Hawk followed. "You know where I come from. Our blood doesn't define us, not since we formed our crew in high school. That's the family I claim. We all do."

My mind whirled. *I can do this.* "I'm counting on that for what I'm about to tell you." I dropped into the chair and met their gazes. "My real name was Max Chavez, before I met all of you. After my parents were murdered, Hugo became my guardian. For six months, we lived in his apartment in New York while he ignored me. At the time, I thought that was the most difficult thing I'd faced."

"That type of abandonment is never easy." There was a kindred soul in Hawk, and I nodded to acknowledge what he'd said.

"Those first few months... I should have run away, and I would have if I'd had any idea what was coming. I should have had a clue that things were going to go to hell when Hugo looked at me for the first time since the day he picked me up from social services. A bag was tossed at my feet that held a few pieces of clothing and nothing else. We boarded a private plane to the Middle East."

The cooling evening air wafting in from the window took on the quality of the desert. My skin crawled as the emotions from those years scratched along every inch of my body: fear, desolation, and finally fury. The last had paid off, but it had taken years.

I wouldn't share the details of my first meeting with Jamal, the leader of the Dark Wings, or what it meant to belong to the organization, to be trained by them, to kill for them, to be owned by them.

To leave had been a death warrant, one they would surely call due.

"My uncle left me there in the desert with a group of mercenaries. I was there for four years. It was... brutal. Death would have been a kindness. That part, Rich cannot know about." I yanked myself from the images and met their gazes, and some of the tension slid away at the resolve I read there. They had my back. I only hoped that would continue when they found out everything.

"How do Kara and Hugo fit in?" Jack asked.

Good. That was better than sifting through memories and deciding what to share. "I met Kara while I lived in the Middle East. Ahmed brought her to be trained so that she wouldn't be a target—and oddly enough, to be his shield."

"He left her there or transported her back for training?" Hawk crossed his arms on the table and leaned forward.

"He struck a bargain with Jamal, and she remained for several months. I never paid too much attention, as her father, Ahmed, was only there at select times and for Kara. My radar consisted mostly of those I dealt with daily."

"So Hugo and Ahmed know one another, are in business together," Jack concluded.

"It appears so. Hugo was tipped off about me by Ahmed. Ahmed learned about me from tapping Kara's phone." *This is so messed up.* "I didn't recognize Hugo that night or from the picture because of the burn scars on the right side of his face, the drooping eyelid, and the beard. I should have."

"It's been twenty-odd years, and it was dark. I can understand why you didn't."

I agreed with Jack, but they needed to know. "The drones in Hugo's hands are a problem, and I would bet he was meeting with Ahmed to sell them to him."

"And if he sells them to Ahmed, since he's one of the Venezuelan president's trusted advisors, we could be facing a terrorist attack." Jack ran his hands through his hair in an angry swipe.

"I'd bet on it." It was going from bad to worse.

"And Kara? Can she be trusted?" Hawk asked.

I wanted to say yes. "I'd like to think so."

"She knew you as Max five years ago in Washington, DC. Wouldn't she have given you away then if she was a risk?"

Hawk brought up a good point, but trusting no longer came naturally to me. I relied on the guys and their wives. No one else made the cut. Aside from our family, I had no use for others. When you'd been burned as badly as I had, letting anyone in was a risk. But Kara had always been a problem for me.

In the dead of night, she'd come to me for protection, and I'd thrown caution to the wind and let her in. Images of the night flooded my memories, and I was at once there again.

———

My eyelids snapped open, and I went from asleep to awake and alert. Darkness permeated the tiny room. I scanned the shadows for threats. Nothing, at least not within those four plaster walls, but something in the hall. Someone was trying to sneak up on me. In my world, that could only mean death. It wouldn't be mine.

Rolling to my feet, I crept to the doorway and flattened against the rough concrete. The noise was barely audible, but I'd learned the hard way to wake ready to fight. My vision adjusted to the small amount of moonlight that filtered from the high, barred window near the ceiling. I could make out a slight form crossing the threshold.

The intruder took one step in, then two. I moved behind and wrapped my hand around the intruder's neck. There was a small, feminine squeak. The scent of lilies swirled in the air. In a quick spin, I shoved her against the wall and pressed a forearm into her windpipe, my knife to the side.

"It's Kara," she rasped.

"Why are you here?" I couldn't trust that she wasn't sent to commit harm.

"I was scared. Some of the others..." Her voice trembled with raw fear. "Around you, I feel safer."

I remembered what it was like when I'd first come to the Dark Wings years before. At fourteen, a year younger than my seasoned fifteen, she was new to the ways of Jamal's mercenary camp. I understood her terror. The unexpected nightly visits were full of torture. They would drag me out of my room, barely awake, only to beat the hell out of me. It taught me to be aware. Vigilant. Then there were the chains. I glanced at her unbound wrists. Our initiations had been very different.

Toward the end of my first year with the sadistic mercenaries, I'd learned some tricks of my own. As I'd grown, I'd become faster, meaner, and more able to predict their next strikes. Then, after the bloodbath that resulted when one of them put their hands on me, they thought twice about those nocturnal visits. At the slightest sound, I would wake, ready to do serious damage.

I understood Kara's predicament. I wasn't sure how much influence or control her father had over the mercenaries there. Jamal's word was law, but there were a few who were evil to the core.

I eased off her, dropping my forearm from her throat, and she sucked in a full, unencumbered breath. Trusting her was a risk. But I'd shown her basic moves earlier that day, and she was inexperienced. I doubted she would be a threat.

Tears welled in her eyes and spilled over her long lashes. My heart squeezed in sympathy—an emotion I was shocked I'd retained. I led her to the corner where I'd been sleeping. The mattress on the ground was a luxury, one I'd earned through blood. After patting her down for weapons—there weren't any—I waved to the makeshift bed. "Sit."

She lowered to the bed and wrapped her thin arms around her tiny waist. Sitting next to her, I sorted through what to say, but she beat me to it.

"One of the trainers told me he looked forward to my first night here. The way he said it..."

Something inside of me flared to life, and the overwhelming need to protect her filled every fiber of my being. Where that'd come from made no sense to me.

I thought Jamal had killed anything decent long before.

I knew who she was talking about, and I would take care of him during sparring the next day. "He can't get to you through me. You'll be safe tonight."

I hoped that I wouldn't come to regret it. But her shell-shocked amber eyes and the tremor that shook her small body imbedded in my conscious. "You have to play the game. During the day, don't let them see you cry. Be tough, no matter what.

They'll try to break you. At night"—what the hell was I doing?
—"I'll keep you safe. Then you can break down if you need to."

On a shaky breath, she inhaled. "Thank you."

"Get some rest."

She stretched out on the mattress, and I did the same, the knife secure in my hand in case anyone entered. Her scent was driving me crazy. How she could smell like lilies in that hellhole was beyond me.

"Is it always like this?" She shifted, turning her head to look at me.

"Like what?" I'd been there for four years. I didn't know anything else.

"Awful. Scary. And... dirty." Raw fear dripped from her voice.

"Yes." That was to put it mildly. "Why are you here?" I didn't understand, as I was ordered to train her for combat.

"My mother died a few months ago. She was murdered. My father is worried I'll suffer the same fate. He told me this is where I'll learn to defend myself."

"This isn't the place for you."

"I don't like it, but I don't want to die."

"That's not what I meant." Our voices were barely above a whisper. "You shouldn't be staying here." I was afraid there was more to the story. "Why would he leave you?"

"He's traveling for business. I'll only be here long enough to learn to fight."

"What's long enough?" I was surprised her father would leave her there. It wasn't safe.

"Four months."

For her, that would be a lifetime. "Get some sleep." As she settled beside me, I couldn't help but consider the time-frame. In five months, I would be leaving against my will with Uncle Hugo. I couldn't let that happen. I had been forming a plan to escape for some time. As her leg pressed against mine and her breathing deepened from sleep, I knew I'd make my exit correspond with hers.

———

I STOOD AGAIN to shake free of the past and jammed my hands into my jeans pockets to keep from punching something. When my fingers curled around something metal, I stopped wearing a path on the floor and pulled it out. A silver locket dangled from a chain in my hand. *What the hell is this?* With care, I pried the two halves of the locket open to reveal a picture of Lily nestled inside.

Lily looked so much like Kara, with her black hair and smooth, tan skin. Her daughter had a sweet smile while Kara embodied exotic dreams, a balm to the senses. She affected me in the way the heat of the day ebbed, ushering in the evening where shadows lengthened, time slowed, and a mix of color smudged across the sky.

Mother and daughter shared the same high cheekbones and perfect mouth. The only difference was their eyes. Kara's were whiskey on a summer's night, framed in smoky lashes. Lily's were the same almond shape with spikey lashes, but the color leaned toward the shade of Samir's hazel ones.

I set the opened locket on the table so the guys could see. "I think we can trust her. Both she and Samir are frantic about Lily."

"We need to get her out, then." Hawk's mouth set in a grim line.

"Agreed." Jack pulled his phone from his pocket. "We

need to agree on what we tell Rich because he will be involved due to the unaccounted-for drones."

The next few minutes consisted of us agreeing on the details—we would share Hugo's involvement with Ahmed. The contract with Samir for Lily's rescue was through Gray Ghost Security and would stay that way, at least for the time being. My history with Hugo, who I suspected was a terrorist, would remain between us.

"Kara said she'd be in town tomorrow." She'd bent over me to whisper for me to find her, and her voice had cut through the haze of the shock of her knifing me. Even though I had understood why she'd done it, my guard would be up when our paths crossed again. "I'll meet with her and find out what our next move is."

10

KEEGAN

WARMTH from the sun heated the bricks on the side of the grocery store that I leaned against. Just out of sight of mainstream foot traffic, I scanned the faces for Kara. I guessed she would get away in the morning, as her words to me about meeting her here had been laced with a frantic edge. The locket and her anxiety over Lily lessened my suspicion and the hatred that had flooded me the first time I'd spoken to Samir. Both parents were on the same page, desperate to protect their little girl.

I eased back an inch, ensuring I couldn't be spotted unless someone neared the narrow alley. The shops in town, if they were still in business, were running on skeleton crews. I'd done my homework. There was a lawyer's office that looked as if it'd had a full crew of ten that was down to one. The restaurant across the way was nearly empty, and the bakery no longer carried flour, effectively halting production. Up the road a mile or so was a neighborhood that was better off than that desolate, politically oppressed area. Most of the people who passed through were on their way to what few jobs were left. Few possessed vehicles. Many walked for miles.

Those who drove vehicles picked up people hitchhiking along the road in what had become ridesharing, as public transportation ceased to exist in many areas or was too dangerous to risk taking. I was pulled from my thoughts as the sound of voices drifted my way. One in particular caught my attention.

Shifting, I gained a view of Kara climbing out of a car along with several others. They were not soldiers or from the wealthy neighborhood where she resided. It seemed the protests didn't extend to Ahmed's daughter. *Does she care about her country?*

The people with her wore baggy clothes that had seen better days. The political turmoil had caused an immense amount of suffering.

The more I scrutinized her actions and their responses, the clearer her intentions were. She cared, and the people knew it, which was why I guessed that the outrage shown at Ahmed's yesterday didn't extend to her. She was greeted favorably in the town rather than accosted.

After she exchanged hugs and offered each person a brown paper bag that looked like a sack lunch, she set out to the string of sparsely populated, if not outright abandoned businesses.

I counted down the seconds until Kara would pass where I waited. *Three. Two. One.* My fingers curled around her bicep, and I pulled her to me. She pivoted and struck at my head with her other hand. I ducked with ease.

Her eyes went wide, and her body visibly relaxed. "I'm sorry."

I brushed aside her apology. It wasn't necessary. What bothered me wasn't that she'd reacted as expected, but what had happened before. "You got the drop on me yesterday. Not many do."

A mischievous grin pulled at her lips, and her amber eyes sparkled with mirth. "I had an incredible teacher."

In accord, we both moved deeper into the shadows the buildings offered. We wouldn't have much time, and I needed to make the most of it, no matter how much Kara distracted me.

Her hand curled around my forearm, halting me from moving back farther, so I shifted us to the side of the building. When I turned, the pain and desperation bleeding from her gaze stopped my heart.

"I need your help, Max."

A spark of fury burned as my given name brought with it a barrage of emotions from the past. "Keegan, not Max. Don't call me that name anymore."

"Okay." Her gaze bounced back and forth between my eyes. "It slipped. It's different and not how I picture you, but I'll remember."

The anger fizzled away, and I smirked. "That was the point."

"Right." She nodded, her gaze sweeping over my long hair. "I need your help. Things at home are escalating, and there are few I trust to get Lily out safely."

"How involved is Ahmed with the Dark Wings?" I used to think he wasn't too deep, but after Hugo showed up, I knew better. Ahmed gave the impression his daughter was there on loan and to learn to fight, whereas Hugo was connected for life.

"He's involved."

It was enough. "Why would you stay with your daughter if he's married to the organization?"

She reared back as if slapped. "You think I wanted my

daughter to grow up in the same household as Ahmed?" Baring her teeth, she whisper-yelled, "He wouldn't let me leave."

I should have walked away, but I couldn't. I knew first-hand what it was like to be a child owned by the organization. "Tell me everything."

"I don't have much time. Ahmed is expecting me back. Lily is in terrible danger, and Samir... I took advantage of his business trip and attempted to fly Lily to him, but Ahmed stopped me. So I set Samir free in the only way I could by telling him not to return. I'd overheard Ahmed mention Samir's usefulness, and it was an indication of the threat here to him, which deepened when I tried to send Lily there."

"Why is Ahmed a danger to Samir? And what's stopping Ahmed from going after Samir?"

"I believe there's a business connection of Samir's he plans to exploit. My husband has been safe until now. Hugo, to my knowledge, is a new associate of Ahmed's, and whatever they are working on together has upped the risk to us all. I can find out what's going on there if that'll convince you to help us."

As if I wouldn't. "I'm in, Kara. But we could use some help. Hugo has possession of small drones. We were sent to retrieve them. Does Ahmed have them?"

"I-I don't know. Hugo was in meetings with my father early yesterday morning. I'll find out whatever I can. Just promise me that you'll get Lily out."

I nodded. "How well do you know Hugo?"

"I only met him once, about a week before I was sent to retrieve whatever possessions he had on him," she explained. "After that initial appointment with Ahmed, something happened. Ahmed was holed up in meetings with the president. Then the company was seized..."

Things were becoming clearer, and I fished for more information. "Hugo must have brokered a deal with Ahmed and the president regarding the drones."

Kara shrugged. "Something must have gone wrong."

"Seems that way, especially because the company was seized shortly after."

Kara pressed her lips into a tight line. "I'm not surprised. My guess is that the president ordered Ahmed to recover the drones and to bypass negotiations with Hugo, who he deemed expendable."

"The kidnapping must have been an unexpected occurrence, then, and not one orchestrated by Ahmed."

She shook her head. "No, Ahmed didn't have anything to do with that. He did learn that Hugo was among the others who'd worked for GH Envirotech. The Americans were supposed to be on their way out of the country."

"That's when you were brought in?"

"Yes. I was sent to retrieve the bag or whatever he had on him."

"You were kept in the dark, then, not told that what you were to recover were insect-sized drones?"

"Exactly."

She'd said she trusted a few people. "The nanny, do you trust her?"

"Yes. Andrea has been with me since Lily was born. She's our best option."

The fact that she used Hugo's name so casually bothered me. "You do know who Hugo is, don't you?"

"Only that he's an associate of Ahmed's."

"He's also my uncle."

"What?" She took a half step back. "I had no idea."

"I shouldn't expect that you would. You never met him when we were at the Dark Wings' camp. He's very dangerous, especially now that he knows I care about you."

Her lips parted, and she sucked in a breath, softening before me.

My fingers curled into a fist, and I fought the urge to touch her, the memory of her soft skin a brand in my mind. I took a step closer.

"You care about me?" Wonder saturated her words as her hand lifted then fell back to her side, inches from resting on my chest.

My fingers uncurled and, seemingly of their own volition, moved toward her hip as my gaze dropped to her lips. I knew how they would taste, how soft her skin was, and the throaty noise she made when she let go. I willed my hand to fall back to my side. We both knew it wasn't the time or the place to get lost in each other.

"Kara"—I couldn't get involved, not with all the uncertainty, regardless of how much I wanted to—"how will you get your daughter to me? If you can do that, I can take her away from here, but you should be with her. It doesn't make sense for you to stay behind."

"We'll see. If I can get away without compromising Lily's safety, I will. For now, let's plan on meeting here tomorrow, in the alley by the boutique. I'll keep tabs on Ahmed and try to get information on the drones."

We came to extract the kidnapped Americans, not knowing one of them was my uncle. That changed things. "Good. The drones do need to be recovered. If you can't get to them, I'll break in."

"No." Her eyes hardened. "That would put Lily in too much danger. I'll do it."

"Fine. You have two days to get any intel you can about

Ahmed and Hugo's meetings, contacts, and most importantly, to recover or locate the drones."

"I told Ahmed you're dead. Hugo should receive the same information."

"If he believes that."

She nodded, her understanding clear in her somber expression. A flash of pain crossed her features, then she reached forward and placed her palm over the concealed knife wound on my chest. "I'm sorry for giving you another scar."

That woman was my kryptonite, and I hoped she wouldn't be the death of me.

11

KEEGAN

I LET myself into the small room we were renting and stopped short when I took in the cell pressed to Jack's ear and the lines of strain around his mouth. Sprawled on the couch, Hawk scrolled on his phone, shedding no light on the cause of Jack's distress.

The door clicked shut behind me, and I waited with my arms crossed over my chest and my feet spread wide. Whatever news he had to share, I had no choice but to wait. He clipped out a response, pressed the speaker option on his phone, then met my gaze. Hawk shifted, his screen no longer holding his attention.

"Rich is on the line." Jack dropped onto one of the chairs near the round table in the middle of the room.

Rich cleared his throat. "Stuart Greene, the Director of National Intelligence Services, collapsed during yesterday's National Security Council meeting. They're determining the cause of death. Until we know for sure, we can't assume it was by foul means. However, another member reported seeing a mosquito on his neck right before he fell to the ground."

"He was known to support the removal of the Venezuelan president," I replied. It sounded like it could have been an assassination to keep Stuart from influencing the vote to add the Venezuelan president to the kill list. "Possibly lethal nanoweapons, then? Seems George could be more involved than he was letting on. Have the recovered hostages been questioned?" His employees could have had vital information that would help us determine if insect nanobots were sold in America through George or only in Caracas. *How is Hugo involved? And is he still here, or did he fly to America with help from Ahmed?*

"Seven days from now, a meeting for the National Security Council is scheduled. We need those drones recovered before then." Rich paused. "I don't think I have to spell out the threat we're facing."

"We'll get it done," Jack responded before disconnecting the call.

"Who from our team is handling interrogations for George Hammond and the recovered employees?" Hawk stood and grabbed one of the protein bars we'd brought with us.

"Mike and Liam are on it. We're to focus on recovering the drones and Henry Adams, aka Hugo Chavez." Jack swiped his cell from the table and shoved it into his front pocket. "Assuming he hasn't fled the country."

"Not likely." My gut said that, unless he'd already left, he wouldn't go anywhere until he was sure, for the second time, that I was dead. "From what I can gather, he's working a deal with Ahmed."

"Will this be a problem with Kara?" Jack's eyebrows rose.

"No. She's going to help in any way she can. Based on how desperate she is to get her daughter out of the country and away from Ahmed, I'd say odds are that we'll find out where the drones are—or at least about any meetings surrounding their purchase—swiftly."

"Since you've been reported as dead"—Jack notched his head in Hawk's direction—"we're heading out to see if we can locate Hugo. The last thing we need is for him to flee the country with nanoweapons. We'll reconvene tomorrow night."

"Keep in touch." Unease skated along my skin, raising the hairs. "And don't let him know you're there. Hugo hasn't made you yet, but if he does, the people he's connected to make me look like a novice."

Hawk and Jack stopped and regarded me for several seconds. I regretted saying what I had, but worry about their safety overruled my desire for self-preservation.

"When are you checking in with Kara?" Jack asked.

"We're meeting tomorrow in town, midmorning." By then, I hoped to have some answers or a sense of direction. Given that she had the same type of training, I had no doubt she would deliver, but I worried regardless. If the heavy hitters from Dark Wings were involved—and by Hugo's presence I guessed they were—she was in danger.

———

Kara

"Mommy!"

I stepped into our family room in the east wing of Ahmed's house, and my heart burst at the sight of Lily running toward me. Her long hair lifted as she ran like a superhero cape wrapped around her head. If only I could make her invincible.

I dropped to my knees, spread my arms wide, then closed them around her when she launched herself at me. I pressed my nose to the spot in between her neck and shoulder and inhaled. To me, she'd retained that innocent, sweet baby smell. Lily was my world. I would do everything in my power to ensure her safety.

"It's time for bed, my sweet." I pulled back enough to ruffle the silky hair on top of her head. "Did you brush your teeth?"

"Uh-huh." She flashed a toothy grin for inspection. "Nanny Andrea already read me a story. Will you tuck me in?"

"Of course, my big girl." I stood and clasped her tiny hand. Her room was next to mine. I wanted to keep her close. Andrea had the one directly across from Lily's.

She crawled into her bed then flopped back against her pillow. I pulled the pink blankets up to her chin. "Snug as a bug?"

"No." A yawn stole any other words she'd planned to say, and I tucked her in loosely, with room to move around as she wanted.

"How were your lessons today?" While she could technically go to preschool, I was worried about sending her, given how hated my father was and his connection to the president. There was no way I would risk Lily incurring any fallout from desperate and impoverished people. I did what I could to help the people of Caracas and would continue to do so. I did not agree with what the government was inflicting on the people.

Because of his position and connections, my father was exempt from experiencing hardship and poverty. I figured he could spare any amount of food I could smuggle out to the villagers as well as rides, clothes—anything I could do to help. Lily yawned, and I focused on her. Our time together was precious, not something I cared to squander with dark thoughts of the state of Caracas.

"Lily, your lessons?" I gently reminded her as she finished another huge yawn.

"Fine."

"Did you like what you were learning?" I had a tutor come for a few hours each day to help her learn to read and basic math, among a spattering of other subjects. She was young but a sponge, and I wanted to take advantage of the time to propel her forward in her studies.

"It was boring."

Hmm, too easy? "Did you already know the answers?"

She shook her head. "No. We did waaay too many numbers."

Math was one of her least favorite subjects. "I'll look over your lessons and see if there is a way to learn them that would be fun."

"'Kay."

I smoothed her hair off her forehead and brushed a kiss there, then on each cheek. "I love you, baby girl."

Her eyelids fell to half-mast. "Not a baby, Mommy."

"Maybe not, but you'll always be mine."

The corners of her mouth lifted in a sweet smile before she gave in and drifted off to sleep. It'd been a long day, and I felt her exhaustion in my bones. Making sure her night-light was on, I turned off the overhead one and closed the door.

Andrea wore a frown when I walked in. Mentally, I prepared for the argument I knew was coming. If she hadn't been a good friend of Mama's, I'd never have put up with her opinions. But Mama was dead, and Andrea was all I had left of her.

I motioned for Andrea to follow me as I sank into the couch, pulling one of the throws around my shoulders. It wasn't cold in there, but I wanted a shield of sorts from whatever she was upset about. I had an idea.

She stood with her arms crossed and that frown chiseled into her pretty features.

"Is something bothering you?" I gave her the opener I knew she was waiting for.

The distance between us closed as she trod across the wood floor with her sensible shoes. Perching on the edge of the couch cushion diagonally from me, she glared. "You know there is, Kara. What is that no-good husband of yours doing out of town? It's been two weeks, and he's yet to return. What does that say to little Lily, hmm?"

"He's working. We've been over this already. I don't understand why you're so upset this time. Samir travels a lot."

"First, you try to send Lily away—"

"To her father!" I threw my hands up in the air.

"You know I don't agree with Samir's business dealings." Andrea's chin angled high. "Consorting with that man in the States."

"He's in business with David Meyer's ancestry company, nothing more." I glared at her to get her to stop. What I said wasn't entirely true, but I would defend Samir with my dying breath.

"And earlier, that horrible man almost abducted Lily."

I narrowed my gaze. Lily wasn't taken away. Ahmed got word and had stopped Andrea and Lily as they walked along the hedge. "What do you know about that man?" I hadn't told her anything yet for fear she would argue and refuse to take Lily to where Max—no, Keegan—was waiting. Worse, I wasn't positive she wouldn't run to Ahmed. It didn't matter, anyway. He'd found out, but I could still plead that it was due to Ahmed taking business meetings too close to my daughter.

Andrea shrugged. "Nothing. Mr. Hernandez told me there was someone spotted on the edge of the lawn and that he'd learned he was after Lily."

She meant well. I knew that. Lily was her world too. I rubbed the bridge of my nose before meeting her gaze again. I had to tell her. Maybe then we would have a chance in hell of getting Lily out of there. "The man was there because I'd asked him to. Ahmed—"

"Why do you call him that? He's your father, Kara." Sadness spread over her features, and she reached out and squeezed my leg.

It was the wrong direction for our conversation to go, but I couldn't brush off her concern. "I'm sorry, Andrea. It's easier for me to call him that because of the business."

She nodded, but the worried frown didn't leave her mouth.

"Ahmed has some business dealings that are dangerous right now."

"It won't always be this way." Removing her hand, Andrea settled on the couch, so her back rested against the cushions. "Lily is safest within these walls."

"I don't think she is." I knew she wasn't. "You know I tried to fly her out to Samir, and Ahmed forbade it. She's *my* daughter." My voice shook at the reminder of the argument I'd had with him that day.

"And *his* granddaughter."

Why? Why does she insist on seeing the good in him? I didn't think any existed anymore, not since Mama died. "I want her to go to Samir for a while. Not forever, but until whatever Ahmed's got going on is wrapped up."

Andrea nodded but didn't look reassured. "What are you planning?"

She was crucial to how I would get Lily out safely. I had to include her, despite the risk she would face if Ahmed caught her. "It's dangerous. If Ahmed learns you're involved, I'm afraid of what he will do."

She sat straight with determination pulling at her features. "For Lily? I would do anything."

That's what I was counting on.

12

———

KEEGAN

NIGHT DESCENDED LOUDLY on the streets below with the sounds of raised voices, tires squealing, and the occasional pop of automatic-weapons fire. Caracas was vastly different than it had been in my youth. Despite how long ago that was, the memories were still fresh.

Jack and Hawk had returned from scouting earlier and were again concealing guns and knives to head out into the night.

"Check in on the hour." With Hugo on the loose and a potential confrontation brewing with members of the Dark Wings, we'd decided that I would continue to lie low. I was doing so for their protection and to feed into the lie Kara had told Ahmed about killing me. At the very least, it bought us a day or two.

"We won't be long." Jack slapped my shoulder as he and Hawk walked past me then out the door.

They were doing surveillance on Ahmed's home in hopes of spotting Hugo. We had to recover the nanoweapons. The loss of the director of National Intelligence Services weighed on us all. Who the next target would be was crucial to identify, as was the drone retrieval. The mission from Rich no longer included recovery of Henry Adams, aka Uncle Hugo.

Everything was moving too slowly and making me jittery, especially since I had yet to discover where Hugo was holed up. I didn't trust that he would believe Kara, and my gut warned that he was double-crossing Ahmed in some way. There would have been no other reason for him to flee when Kara approached.

Despite my best defenses, remaining behind opened the door for my mind to dredge up past horrors, particularly my introduction to the Dark Wings. I rubbed my eyes, trying to stave off the memory, but it came barreling through my head as violently as they had.

I was eleven. The hot, dry wind of the Sahara slapped my face, robbed my eyes of moisture, and leeched my mouth of saliva. Six long months had passed in my uncle's care, if it could be called that.

Abandonment had a distinctly bitter taste. Standing next to him, overlooking an open expanse where men sparred on ground packed from the tread of feet and impact of bodies, I had a sixth sense I would experience that particular condition yet again.

It'd been six months since my parents passed away from the car accident.

In my uncle's care, I had ceased to exist until the day before.

Our plane had touched down hours ago, and he had only said a handful of words to me. Among them were "duty," "birthright," and "what is owed." As I stood in front of a giant of a man dressed in black robes and with a turban on his head, I began to understand.

With my hands fisted by my side, I waited for what

disaster would befall me next. I didn't have long to wait.

"This is the boy?" The large man with coal for eyes looked me over and seemed to take my measure.

A mixture of anger and fear collided as I held his gaze without flinching. I knew their language fluently, but he spoke in English for my benefit. I'd let him assume that's all I understood. Somehow, I knew I had to keep as much of myself as possible secreted away.

My uncle handed my small duffel to an angry-looking man who came forward then turned to me. I didn't want to break eye contact with the giant, but my uncle's fingers bit into my shoulder, so I turned to him.

"This is your birthright. Do as you're told and become a weapon."

No. Something is very wrong here. "You're leaving me here?"

There was no emotion on his face, and I worked hard to wipe the despair that bubbled up from my features as well. "I'll return for you after your sixteenth birthday, when you're useful."

What does that even mean?

I snapped out of the memory, fighting the urge to purge the water I'd consumed from my stomach. I'd learned exactly what that meant moments after Hugo had left and each day from then on. The bruises I'd worn as tattoos beneath my skin had been a reminder, the scars etched in my back and various other places more permanent. Hugo had delivered me into hell, but I'd crawled out before he was able to collect me.

Jack and Hawk might have been out there gathering intel, but after I met with Kara, I would hunt down Hugo and teach him exactly what I had become, what his investment all those years ago had made me.

13

KARA

WITH LILY safely tucked into bed for the night, I was free to check on Ahmed. Not only did I owe Keegan, but I trusted him with Lily, and I was desperate to get her away from what was going on. If Andrea wanted to go, too, I would arrange it. No one was safe under the same roof as Ahmed. I'd learned that when I was young.

On the other side of the house, in the west wing, my shoes made no sound on the thick carpet. No one roamed there. A few more steps, and his office was in sight, the door shut tightly. A sliver of light spilled from beneath the threshold and into the dimly lit corridor.

I rubbed my damp palms along the sides of my jeans. Pressing against the wall, I held still and listened. The murmur of voices, too soft to clearly understand, drifted into the hallway. I caught a word here and there, but that was it. "Causing trouble... eliminate... two days" was all I could make out, but it was enough. The timeline for whatever he was ordering was in two days' time. I steeled myself, took a deep breath, then rapped my knuckles on the door.

Talking came to a halt, and not two seconds later, the

door was yanked open. I blinked to adjust to the bright interior.

"What is it?" Ahmed growled.

I infused calm into my posture despite the mixture of rage and fear building to a crescendo in me. "What is this meeting about?" I leaned to the right, past Ahmed, to see who was within the room.

Oh no. Instinctually, I wanted to take cover from whom I'd glimpsed, but I forced my feet to grow roots. The person he was meeting with was none other than the leader of the Dark Wings, Jamal. He'd terrified me when I was younger. Nothing had changed since.

Ahmed's thick brows rose, and a mocking smirk replaced the frown he'd worn a minute ago. "You want to be included in this meeting?" He took a step to the side, and Jamal got to his feet. The scar that marred his cheek made him even more frightening somehow. "I seem to remember, before Lily was born, pressing you to take an interest and you adamantly not wanting any involvement. Why now?"

This is for Lily. The shield I'd plastered on my face stayed strong. I wouldn't let them see my fear. For my daughter, I would endure anything. "It's time, don't you think?" I mirrored Ahmed's frown. "You have me run missions for you and do your dirty work but keep me from the heart of the business? The profits? The inner workings? I'm your daughter." I notched my chin higher. They respected strength, cunning, and greed. "It is my birthright to be equal in your dealings, to share in the profits."

"You are a girl. Why could you possibly think you have a seat in my arena?"

I met Ahmed's challenge head-on. "A girl who has taken down assassins for you and who has completed every mission but one that you've sent me on. I am more than capable and a worthy adversary. It would be better to have me at your side than not."

The threat hung between us while I witnessed a range of emotions bleed through Ahmed's eyes—first fury, then my death, and finally, cunning acceptance. "Very well. Come in, *daughter*."

I inclined my head as I entered the snake pit despite the mocking tone in his voice. In time, that would be dealt with. After a curt nod to acknowledge Jamal, I stood behind the chair to his right, my hands grasping the strong frame. I wouldn't sit and put myself at a disadvantage. Ahmed shut the door and rounded the desk to take his seat. As Jamal lowered himself, I did too. Arms loose at my sides, I was hyper-focused on Jamal in case he decided to strike.

Memories of my time training with him after Keegan's escape threatened to dismantle the tight control I had on my mind. Slamming up against an internal wall, I concentrated on Ahmed's words and did everything I could to block the onslaught of terror that Jamal evoked in me.

It wasn't the first time he'd been there. Ahmed hired him from time to time. Even so, my interactions with him had been limited, and I preferred it that way.

I would let the emotions out later if I must, but not just then. It would only have sealed my fate in the worst way possible, and that would not have helped Lily. No one spoke, which I found odd.

I waited another second then laid my cards on the table, since it was apparent that's what Ahmed wanted. "What was in the backpack you wanted so badly, and have you recovered it since that night?" Refusing to acknowledge Jamal, I kept my gaze locked on Ahmed.

"The pack you failed to retrieve?"

Jamal was quiet, and for that, I was grateful. If I only had to deal with Ahmed for the next few minutes, I might survive the conversation. "There were extenuating circumstances. We've already discussed this."

"It's interesting that you failed to tell me that Max was a part of that equation."

At the mention of Max, Jamal's head swiveled my way, and I felt the cold burn of his dead gaze. "The hostage escaped with the pack while Max kept me occupied."

They were unaware that I'd learned the hostage was Hugo, Keegan's uncle, and I wasn't about to tell them. "Maybe they were working together?" I volleyed back at him. They weren't, but I would use any way I could to gain information.

"I find that interesting. Isn't Max the person you and your husband were working with to take my granddaughter from me?"

Bastard. I wanted to tear him apart with my bare hands. He would not do to Lily what he'd done to me. I would see him dead before I let that happen. "She is *my* daughter, and I was trying to send her to her *father,* which you assumed you had a right to forbid. I did not know that the man Samir hired to help us was Max." I sucked in air and fought to regain control of my emotions and the conversation. "What was in the backpack? And who was the man who got captured in the first place?" I pushed for any tidbit of information they might share so I could turn around and tell Keegan. There could have been new intel of benefit to him and his team.

"It's irrelevant to you as plans are already in motion, and the hostage in question agreed to work with me despite your failed efforts." Ahmed nodded toward Jamal, indicating he was taking over that particular operation. "However, if you insist on being more involved, I will endeavor to find work for you."

"You're missing the point." I delivered my words in the same cold manner, spiced with malice, that he had. "I deserve to be brought into the fold, fully."

"Perhaps, in time. But what I will do is share with you that we're expecting a guest tomorrow evening. You may sit in on that meeting."

"Who is the guest?" Ahmed's dark eyes gleamed with malice, and I steeled myself against whatever he had up his sleeve, because it was definitely something. When he looked at me like that, he always had ulterior motives.

"Hugo Chavez."

"Max's uncle?" Maybe I was mistaken and he didn't have anything up his sleeve. Maybe. Regardless, it was news I could relay.

"Yes. In the meantime"—Ahmed's gaze narrowed—"it seems your skills are lacking, as you failed to eliminate your adversary."

"I did the second time he came around." He couldn't possibly know that Keegan had lived. I'd bribed the guard with a large sum of money to report to Ahmed that he had disposed of the body. "He's dead."

"So you say." Ahmed and Jamal exchanged a look that said they were exploring that detail. "Do not cross me, Kara. Ever. Or you'll end up with the same fate as your mother."

Ice spiked my blood. "What—?"

"Jamal will give you a refresher course so you will not fail again." Ahmed rose, dismissing us.

The horror over working closely with Jamal for the next however many hours that night was overshadowed by the bomb Ahmed had dropped. *Did he kill my mother?*

14

KARA

I THREW the Jeep into Park and plastered a smile on my face for the four people I'd driven into town. As I hugged each one, I tucked some money into their pockets and whispered that the time was nearing. They knew. On one of the many trips I'd made with a large rotating group of villagers, I'd shared that there would be a day when I might have to leave. They understood. Ahmed's cruelty was known far and wide. I tried to do what I could for them—they were my people too.

What clothes, food, ridesharing, and whatever money I could smuggle from Ahmed, I passed on to them. I gave them all I could, and I had enough cash squirreled away in an offshore account for Lily and me if we got away. Aside from that, I shared almost all the allowance he gave me to those in need. Mom had set up the secret account for me before she died, and I wondered whether that was why she'd been killed. I had a feeling there was more to the story than I was aware, but nothing could have shocked me at that point.

With a last squeeze to the seventy-year-old woman with white hair wrapped haphazardly atop her head, I made my way to Keegan. Meeting him was a huge risk, especially after what had happened the night before.

I inhaled shallow breaths so as not to aggravate my bruised ribs, courtesy of Jamal. That wasn't all. The only thing he'd spared had been my face. The rest of my body was black and blue. The reason behind the abuse was simple: Ahmed instructed Jamal to ensure that I was too sore to escape.

I would have liked nothing more than to down heavy, mind-numbing painkillers, but I couldn't afford to have a fuzzy mind or slow reactions. Discipline kept me from hunching over or limping. Showing pain was a weakness.

I hurried along the sidewalk while scanning my surroundings for anything out of the ordinary. There was a good chance that one of Jamal's men was waiting for me, thanks to Ahmed. Because of that, I went into the clothing store, which was still in business only because of my insistence that Ahmed ensure they had government support, so I could buy clothes for Lily and myself.

Bells jingled above the door as I entered. Maria rushed around the counter, a smile on her lean face.

"Good morning."

"Kara, it's so good to see you." She wrung her hands, her features strained.

"Is everything all right?" My body tensed, ready for anything.

After a few vigorous nods, she ventured closer. "Yes. A large man was in here earlier. He didn't say anything but checked the dressing rooms and the back area too."

Good. Jamal or one of his men would think the store was

safe and that I wasn't doing anything more than shopping. "They shouldn't be in again." I clasped her hands in mine. "Please try not to worry, but I need you to do something for me and not to speak of it if asked."

"Of course. Anything."

I knew she would have my back, as her store had been in dire straits until I'd intervened. "Please gather and ring up a week's worth of new clothes for both Lily and me, and then I need you to bring mine to the dressing room as if I'm trying them on. Then take some out and bring more, as if I'm busy shopping."

"As if you are in there?" Her brows furrowed, and she smoothed her hair while her gaze darted around.

"Maria, it'll be fine. No one will suspect a thing. I'm going to slip out the back for a few minutes while you have the dressing room door open." It would block my escape and subsequent reentry.

"Let's start with these shirts." I gathered a few and brought them back to the changing room. She followed and chatted as if everything was normal. I hung the tops as she looked inside and then slipped away. I heard the click of the dressing room door as I snuck out the back. Jamal wouldn't have seen the door—we kept it hidden by a large dumpster out back, and both inside and out, boxes blocked the area. There was a very narrow space I could maneuver through.

I didn't have long. Keegan was in the recessed alcove I'd indicated yesterday. I snuck behind him with care, making enough noise for him to hear me. My heart fluttered as it always did around him. As a girl, I'd had such a crush on him. Then there was our single night together, when I'd managed to elude Ahmed while he was in meetings. Keegan had ruined me for all others, not that there would be any.

Has he found the locket yet?

"What's wrong?" Keegan growled.

Those green eyes of his burned into me, harvesting my secrets. I shrugged, concentrating on moving languidly, but it didn't matter because he already knew. With care, he edged my shirt away from my neck to bare my shoulder and the bruising that marred it. I stepped back, even though I would have preferred to lean into his touch. "It's nothing."

"Doesn't look like nothing, Kara."

"You of all people should understand." I waited for his reluctant nod. "None of that matters, though. What does is Lily. Come tonight. I'll leave the third window on the ground floor, east side and to the rear, unlocked. There will not be an alarm. The guards are on a seven-minute rotation. Eleven o'clock. Show her what I gave you, and she'll go without a fuss."

"What you gave me?"

Men. "I hid my locket in your pocket the day I stabbed you. Lily will know it's from me." Both exasperated and nervous, I shook my head. "You're slipping."

"I did find that, and you'd stabbed me. I chose not to retaliate." He pressed his mouth into a hard line.

I fought the urge to roll my eyes. "Like you could've." I chuckled under my breath. "Ahmed is meeting with Hugo tonight, and I'm worried about the possibility of my father hurting Lily, or me in front of her." I jerked forward a half step, barely stopping myself from touching him. I needed the connection, the assurance he would help us. "Get her out, Keegan. Take her to Samir."

"I don't like you there. Come with me when I get Lily." He lifted a piece of my dark hair and rubbed it between his thumb and index finger.

My concentration wavered, and I swayed toward him. I couldn't leave yet. "No. I need to make sure Ahmed is occupied, that Lily can get away safely."

"I don't like it."

"Me neither, but it's what we have to do. I won't risk him stopping her escape or worse. Take Andrea with you too."

"The nanny? Will she be in the same room?"

"The same wing. Andrea will help to calm Lily. I'll tell her I need her to stay close. She'll understand because I've shared with her that I'm to sit in on a meeting I'm not comfortable with." I hesitated. I would have told her, but the worry that she would let it slip to Ahmed was real. "She won't know about the plans for tonight."

Seconds ticked by, and I fought the urge to shift from foot to foot. He was very intense, and I longed to lean against him, thread my fingers into the soft hair that fell in loose curls around his sinfully attractive face, and once more let him shoulder my fears and pain.

He closed the distance between us and brushed a kiss along my cheek. Awareness and desire hit me hard. I wanted to press myself against him and accept what he would give. It took everything I had not to turn my head and offer my lips. But there was Samir...

"Thank you." I cupped the side of his jaw, and his stubble teased my skin. "I'll do everything I can to get what Hugo is bargaining for with Ahmed, but I need you to get Lily out no matter what."

"If Hugo hasn't sold the drones to Ahmed yet, my guess is that he will tonight."

"I'll handle it. Just promise me one thing." Too much time had passed, and I needed to get back into the shop and have Jamal or his men see me leaving with bags of clothing. "If you don't see any of Jamal or Ahmed's men, I need you to go into this store through the back and take the bags Maria has for Lily. There are clothes in there for her to wear during the extraction."

"I'll get her out." His features hardened. "Then I'll be back for you."

15

KEEGAN

After texting Jack and Hawk, I wove through back alleys until I was far enough away from where Kara and I had been. No one met my gaze, and I tried to tone down the sense of dread that urged me to break into a sprint. The afternoon sun beat down on my bowed head. There wasn't much farther to go. Two more blocks, and I'd be at the side entrance to the small inn where we were renting a room.

I had to see the locket again. There had been something in her voice that said it was important. Jack had balled up my shirt and tossed it in the bathroom, as there was blood all over it. We'd looked at the pictures, then I'd shoved the necklace back into my pocket. Later, I'd kicked the bloody jeans somewhere. I hoped I hadn't lost it.

I slipped through the doorway and hurried to our room. It was like stepping into a sauna. The air was thick, stagnant. Before I did anything, I opened the windows. A warm breeze stirred the air, offering some relief.

I dropped the bag of clothes Kara had arranged for me to pick up from the store then got to work. It didn't take long to locate my jeans in the corner of the room. When my fingers met the small piece of jewelry, I dropped back to the floor. The small gold heart dangled from the chain. With care, I opened it to study the two pictures inside with new eyes. One was of Kara holding a newborn. Wisps of her black hair clung to her neck, and a smile of joy stretched her full lips, transforming her from gorgeous to a goddess.

The other picture was of Lily, and it seemed current, based on what I knew of Kara's daughter, which wasn't much more than she was four years old. She looked exactly like her mother with long, black hair and high cheekbones. Her eyes, though, were not Kara's. My heart rate spiked. Samir's had a similar shade to Lily's, but not quite. Those eyes stopped my heart. I knew them. I'd known them forever.

What the hell is going on, Kara?

With the necklace looped over my hand, I covered my face while memories slammed home. Five years dissolved, and I was back in DC, reuniting with Kara after a lifetime.

The bar was dimly lit, and all I wanted to do was drink a whiskey and decompress after the mission we'd completed. At least that was the plan until I saw her beneath the glow of a streetlight. It didn't take long until she was inside. An airy sundress floated around her long legs. The same long black hair spilled over her shoulders. I wanted to wrap it around my fist. I couldn't believe she was the same girl who had curled next to me on that ratty mattress on a dusty floor smack in the middle of hell. She'd grown up. Every bit of her was curvy seduction and perfection. My blood heated as I imagined her crawling into my bed. My gaze crawled over her full deep-red lips and that stunning face, which I'd never fully exorcised from my mind.

She made her way to the bar and placed her order. Her

eyes were downcast, reading something on her phone as I stood.

"Ankara," I murmured loud enough for her to hear me from where I sat in the corner. Not her name, but a nickname that only I'd used on occasion when I'd trained her years prior. It was something no one else knew about, just a made-up connection between us.

For a millisecond, her arm froze, her wineglass halfway to her mouth as she met my gaze in the mirror behind the bartender. She took a sip before setting the glass down then turned to face me.

"Are you here for me, Max?" Steely determination and a healthy dose of fear swam in her eyes.

"Not in the way you're thinking." *Max.* God, it'd been so long since I'd been called that. To see her again... Part of me was glad we weren't flying back to Maine until the next day. The rest of the guys had turned in. I couldn't sleep, and I was glad for the insomnia, as it'd brought her. "What are you doing here? In America?"

A half smile curved her lips. "My father had some business, and I tagged along. Is this where you live now? Where you went after..."

"I just finished a job." Telling her was a big risk, but I wasn't picking up on anything that would cause a problem for me. "I go by Keegan now."

"Mysterious." She eased back in her seat. "New name and I'm guessing a new mission, based on the clothes you're wearing?"

I wore my military pants. It wasn't a stretch for her to figure it out. "Legit job. We primarily do rescue and recovery."

"Want to get out of here?" Her eyes sparkled with

mischief, and she trailed her fingers along my forearm. "And catch up? Or... go back to where you're staying?"

I got up because there was no way I was letting her walk out of there alone tonight. From what I knew about that girl —*woman*—she'd had a crush on me back then, at least as much as was possible in the situation we'd been in. Unless I was reading her wrong, her interest had remained. Her head reached the top of my shoulder as we turned to go, and my hand settled on the small of her back.

It wasn't long before we were at my hotel. There was no way I would go to wherever she was staying and risk running into her father or anyone else from my past. As soon as we were behind the door, I ran my hands along her sides until I reached the hem of her dress. There were some things I couldn't ignore, and the possibility of hidden weapons was a very real scenario.

Her palm pushed against my chest. "Why don't we make this easier for ourselves?" She turned, giving me her back.

I lifted her hair and moved it to the side as her heated gaze met mine over her shoulder. I slid the zipper down and revealed the gentle slope of her toned back in tantalizing increments. I eased the straps from her shoulders, and her dress dropped and pooled around her feet. A gun was strapped to her thigh, as well as a knife. She removed them and set them aside.

Goddamn. She'd filled out. I complied and yanked my shirt off. The little gasp that escaped her parted lips did a lot to ease my discomfort about how much I'd already fallen under her spell. She shimmied out of her underwear then did a slow turn, lifting her hair when her back was to me before we faced one another again—there were no additional weapons.

I divested myself of my gun and dropped my pants. Left in tight black boxer briefs, I held still for a fraction of a second. I didn't turn as she had because I wasn't about to give anyone my back. Removing our guns and knives only eliminated some of the worry. We were both weapons. I would have to wait and see if I'd find out just how deadly her skills were.

I crowded her against the door and bent enough to kiss the hollow between her neck and shoulder. My palm cupped her hip, and her arms went around my waist. I kept enough distance between us to do what I wanted. Threading my fingers through her hair, I trailed kisses, tugging gently on the strands at her nape for greater access. The breathy sigh she made stirred my blood hotter—*this woman.*

My hands slid down to grasp her toned ass before lifting her. Her legs automatically wrapped around me. Then her arms wound around my neck, and our lips met in a frenzy of need. I wouldn't be able to wait much longer—she was a drug that I couldn't resist, and with a strength that surprised even me, I broke our kiss. Our lips were an inch apart. I couldn't have moved away if I'd wanted to.

Close to the bed, I laid her down. I followed and covered her with my weight, maintaining our eye contact.

"Are you sure about this?" I had to make what it was clear because she mattered. "I can't make you any promises."

"Shh." A long finger rested on my lips, and a curtain of black hair fanned across the pillow. "I'm more than sure."

A haze of lust coated my vision as I cupped her breast. She fit perfectly in the palm of my hand, and I gently squeezed while my mouth lavished attention on her other one. I tugged at her nipple with my teeth, and she arched, giving me greater access. Every inch of her body was firm and toned, her olive skin soft and inviting.

She was mine for the night, and I was going to do everything to her that I wouldn't allow when we were together and my role was that of a protector. I wouldn't break her trust then. But that night, she'd initiated, and I planned on fulfilling her every fantasy.

I kissed my way down her abdomen, her breathy moan music to my ears. Parting her toned thighs, I nipped the inside of her leg. She was so beautiful, writhing beneath my touch, pulling me closer to mindless desire. Our heated gazes caught and held as her fingers grasped my hair and she tugged. The sharp tingles along my scalp from her urgency unleashed my own. "I want to taste you," I whispered.

"Later."

Moving over her, I hovered between her legs, dipping to her neck as her fingers curled around me, guiding me inside her warmth. Our bodies fit perfectly together, and it was a reminder of what we'd had when we were young, with unfulfilled sexual tension that became a live wire between us. We finally had our chance, and we were both desperate for it.

At her touch, my control snapped, and I thrust home. She moved to match my rhythm, and I invaded her mouth with my tongue. Her nails bit into my skin as she demanded more. I would give her anything—anything I could.

The first time was fast and desperate.

I took my time with her the second time and the third. Slipping my hand between us, I circled her swollen nub, teasing her until she arched and cried out. Only then did I allow myself to give in, to follow her into oblivion. A shudder jolted my body at her heat, and my hands curled, needing her with every fiber of my being. Once with her would never be enough.

A door slammed behind me, and I jumped to my feet. The dingy room in Caracas came back into focus along with Jack and Hawk. I swallowed past the lump in my throat, the feel of Kara's skin still on the tips of my fingers and flooding my senses.

"You okay?" Hawk moved around Jack and came closer.

I shoved him back, still trying to make sense of reality, as it had come crashing into the one from my night with Kara. I opened my palm and let the locket dangle between us. No, I was not okay. We'd used a condom the first time. Not the second. *She hadn't told me.* The fact that she had indirectly, years later and via a picture, did little to quell the sense of betrayal that paved the initial way.

Lily is mine.

FEW LIGHTS WERE on as Jack, Hawk, and I maneuvered through the neighborhood where Ahmed resided. His home was offset from all the others. With his political connections, that wasn't surprising. Men with machine guns stood at their posts along the third-story balcony while guards walked the perimeter, passing us in seven-minute intervals.

We were early. They would not expect us to enter where we planned to if we were to attack. Kara and Lily had the east wing, and we weren't breaching that section, as it would be heavily guarded. To throw them off, we crouched on the adjacent side of the home, but not Ahmed's wing. That would also have been expected. Within the surrounding foliage, we got comfortable to wait until it grew closer to the time Kara had specified.

Before we'd left, each of us had triple-checked our bags. We all had med kits equipped for any emergency, including triage. Saline, antibiotics, and surgical tools were a necessity when we couldn't get to a hospital or doctor. And given the risk Lily would face when we escaped, we'd ensured that we were prepared for every possible scenario.

My emotions were a bundle of uncertainty where Lily was concerned, but it was no place to entertain anything other than a high-level focus on getting the job done. I had to think of her as any other rescue mission, not my potential daughter. Locking down the questions, I scanned the area, including behind me, accounting for the rotating guards and any potential unknown variable.

Jack tapped his wrist. We were going in. Under the cover of darkness, we ran across the lawn as the rooftop guard on our side turned to scan the opposite area. There would be only a handful of seconds. At top speed, we barely made it. If we hadn't, Hawk would've taken care of the threat with the precision of the sniper that he was.

Pressed flat against the stucco, we waited several minutes for the rooftop guard to finish his rotation above then moved to the designated window. There would only be one minute until the perimeter guard rounded the corner. Hawk squeezed my shoulder, and I did the same to Jack, letting each know we were good to go. Jack took off at a fast pace, and we followed. On the side of the house that Kara and Lily occupied, we neared the entry point.

I counted off the windows and found the one Kara said would be open. The guys knew we were to take the nanny with Lily if she was there. It was risky enough trying to get the little girl out—so many things could go wrong.

In record time, we climbed through the window and closed it, so no one was aware of our entry. The hallway was dark, and we would have to navigate to her room. I was surprised we hadn't run into a problem with at least one of the guards. However, they were on high alert and congregated more toward the front of the house, where protests or potential threats were known to happen, as we'd witnessed the day Kara stabbed me.

The house was eerily quiet. Deceptively so. Kara was in a late-night meeting with Hugo. The unpredictability of the situation didn't sit right with me, and being so close by, I had to work to stay focused. But the little girl was the priority. I could return to kill Hugo another day.

Hardwood flooring stretched down the hallway. We stepped with care while keeping a brisk pace. The door was in sight. We were to enter the fourth on the left. I'd taken the lead. My hand curled around the handle, and with a click, we were in. A soft glow emitted from a corner lamp, providing enough light to see there was no one inside. With the drapes drawn, we stood a chance of not being detected from outside—*thank you, Kara.*

We passed through the living room, rounded the plush crème couch, and headed down the side hallway where the bedrooms were. The third on the right was Lily's, across from the nanny's. Kara's was at the end. Jack opened the nanny's door, Hawk remained in the hall, and I pushed open the one to Lily's room.

A nightlight glowed in the corner. After a quick scan for hidden threats or toys in my path, I went to the twin bed, which had a small bump in the middle. A princess canopy of pink encased the mattress, and gauzy fabric draped the sides but was held back with ties.

Chills broke out all over as I looked down at the little angel sleeping. Dark hair spilled across her pillow. Long eyelashes kissed her plump cheeks, and her perfect bow-shaped mouth was parted in sleep. She was a doll-sized version of her mother. I wished there could have been another way for us to meet for the first time.

I pulled Kara's necklace from my pocket, opened the locket, and dangled it in front of her face in preparation. This part was going to suck. Covering her mouth with my large hand, I whispered by her ear in Spanish, "Lily, I need you to wake up."

Her eyelids fluttered, and she stirred beneath my hand. I could sense the scream building as her body tensed, and her eyes widened to saucer size. "Don't make a noise. Your mom sent me."

I shifted the locket, drawing her gaze from my frightening army paint to the delicate jewelry.

I had to grit the next part through my teeth, but she wouldn't know who I was. "Remember, she tried to send you to your dad?"

Her gaze locked back on mine—the same eyes. She gave a tiny nod, and the panic ebbed from her features, curiosity stealing its place.

"I'm going to take my hand away. Will you stay quiet?"

Again, she nodded.

"If we make any noise, your grandfather will stop us, and that'll make your mom very upset."

Through the eyes of a child, I lost my heart. She gazed back at me with the wisdom of one much older. I thought she would've been sheltered, but she must have seen things that alerted her to danger.

Slowly, I removed my hand and gave her the most reassuring look I was capable of. "There are two other men with me. Don't be afraid, Princess. Your mom knows they're helping too. Think of us as knights saving you from the castle dragon."

A small smile curved her cherubic face, and she reached

for me with tiny arms. *God, what I wouldn't do for this child or her mother. This changes everything.* After making sure Lily was safe, I would return for Kara.

I lifted her small weight into my arms then crept to the doorway to find Hawk and Jack waiting for me. They smiled at Lily as she clung to my neck. It was chilly outside, and she wore a sleeveless nightgown. I set her on her feet and pulled out the pint-sized sweater and a small blanket I'd stashed in my pack. I was glad I had. There wasn't much I could do about her lack of socks and shoes. Hawk had the rest of her things from the store in the car and would help her when he could.

I raised my eyebrows to Jack, not wanting to mention the nanny in case that upset Lily. He shook his head no. She was supposed to be there. That she wasn't could pose a problem. I shut Lily's door behind me with a quiet click, and we maneuvered through the hallway and into the main living space.

Hawk took point, and Jack covered my back. I whispered to Lily, "Stay very quiet and hide under the blanket, all right?"

She nodded, and I tucked the blanket over her head, doing my best to make her look like a bulky front pack rather than a small child clinging to my chest. I pulled out my gun since she couldn't see it, but I knew she would feel it. With my hand holding my weapon, I used the same arm to press lightly against her head to keep her body secure. My other arm was beneath her and held her weight as we entered the hallway.

Voices carried, but they were far enough away that we had time, I hoped. Hawk sprinted down the hall, and Jack and I followed. Hawk had the window up and the area scanned in record time. We slipped through the first-story opening and lowered the window back down. Low flowering bushes surrounded the house, and we spaced out into a line and lay flat just as the perimeter guard came into view.

Lily cuddled against my chest and the building. I lay on my side but angled over her, creating a human shield should shots fire. Seconds passed before Jack nudged my leg, and I rolled to my feet. Lily clung to me like a tiny monkey, making no noise and not moving. Her quick acceptance of the situation and her body language made me wonder what exactly she had lived through to understand the importance of staying silent.

We sprinted at top speed through the grass. A silenced pop sounded behind me as Hawk and Jack switched positions in our lineup. I knew what that meant. Someone had spotted us, and one of my teammates had taken care of it—there was no time to look. Our strides lengthened, and we closed in on the foliage where we'd cut the fence. Jack darted through the bushes, and I heard the links whine back as he pulled them open.

Hawk flanked my left, but movement from my right side sent a jolt of adrenaline through me, and my hand left Lily's head to aim at the guard who had spotted us. As he raised his arm and opened his mouth to alert the others via a mic, I fired. He dropped as Hawk and I cleared the bushes then the fence.

16

KEEGAN

WE KEPT OUR PACE UP, never slowing. With two down, the rest of the guards would soon be alerted to the intrusion. Jack had arranged for a vehicle, but it wouldn't appear until we cleared another few blocks. Lily's spare clothes were in there. Hawk would take her back. I trusted the guys with my life—and with my daughter's.

"Over there!" Shouts ripped through the air.

Bullets whizzed by us. *What the hell?* They knew we had Lily and risked her safety by shooting. Jack and Hawk fired a few rounds behind us, but we had to keep moving. If we stopped, there would be more men, and our chances of getting Lily to safety would diminish.

Jack veered right around a corner. I followed with Hawk behind me. Heat from a bullet blasted my calf. *Godammit.* I didn't think it hit me, but it was hard to tell. Didn't matter. I increased my speed. If we could get to the car before more joined them, we would be golden.

Air sawed in and out of my lungs as I pushed to move faster. Lily stayed silent, her little fingers and knees digging into me. It was a relief rather than a hindrance. *A few more feet.*

The neighborhood was dark, foreboding. Eyes would peer through cracks in the drapes, but no one interfered. A deep-seated hatred for the government would tie their tongues. Not many knew we were there, but those who did were loyal to Kara and all she did for them.

I knew better than to let the relief of seeing our way out inhibit the urgency with which we fled. At any moment, all hell could have broken loose. Sweat dripped down my back, and I prayed for Lily's safety to a God I hadn't spoken to for many dark years.

The Jeep was without a cover, the bars wrapped in foam. Jack jumped into the driver's seat. Hawk took the passenger's, and I launched myself into the back with Lily. As the motor roared to life and we jerked forward, I uncovered her head. Jack didn't waste a second. We sped forward as the men who pursued us rounded the corner.

It was one of the only times I had to reassure her. When the blanket cleared her head, she lifted her red-tinged face to me, strands of dark hair sticking to it. I brushed the hair away. Again in Spanish, even though Kara said she spoke English fluently, I told her what to expect. I offered her the comfort of the language spoken most in her home to ease some of her fears.

"My name is Keegan, and I've known your mom since she was a teenager. Don't be afraid, okay?" I slipped the locket over her head so she could have a piece of her mom with her for comfort.

"Where is my mommy?"

"She stayed behind so your grandfather didn't suspect anything." She had to have known he wasn't a good man.

"I want her." She blinked at me without even a hint of

tears. Again, the eyes—they were slaying me.

If only I could've gotten Kara out at the same time to ease this transition for Lily. "I'm staying behind for her, Lily. I'll get her out safe and to you soon. You're going to go to America with my friend Hawk." I pointed to him.

"Where Papa is?"

"Yes. Hawk will take care of you until your mom is there too."

She nodded then rested her head on my chest, and I fought an onslaught of emotions. It wasn't far from the boat. We had it well hidden, as there was no way we could have entered the country legally.

A half an hour later and with luck on our side, we were almost upon the little alcove where I would part ways with both Lily and Hawk. Jack would remain to help with Kara's extraction and the drones—we still had to retrieve those.

Several minutes later, the Jeep jerked to a stop, dirt and sand rising like a cloud around us. Hawk jumped out while Jack remained at the wheel, his gun out and ready. I sat up and handed Lily to Hawk then got out too. Her gaze clung to me for an overlong moment before she looked to Hawk. When he got her to Aruba, a helicopter would take them to an airstrip that housed the jet we'd flown in on. Hawk would take her to the girls, who would spoil her rotten, and alert Samir. There was no way I was okay with her leaving, though. I'd made that clear to the guys. But everything would get straightened out when Kara and I returned home.

My fingers brushed her cheek in a soft caress. "Listen to Hawk. He'll get you away from here and to your dad. I'm going to bring your mom very soon."

I handed her over, and she nodded as she clung to Hawk. "Hurry."

"I'll do my best, Princess."

17

KARA

BRIGHT LIGHT FILLED Ahmed's office as I stood across from him, working hard to keep my features blank. It was late, and we were supposed to have a meeting with Hugo. It was the perfect time to put my plan into motion for Lily and to help with locating the drones.

In appearances, we didn't look like father and daughter. For that, I was glad. His face was round where mine was oval. We both had high cheekbones, but that was our only remote similarity.

I glanced at my watch, under the guise of the meeting rather than my anxiety over the plot I'd concocted to free my daughter from my father. Keegan should have been on the premises, and every muscle in my body strained as I hoped he would get Lily out safely.

"He's late." A few minutes past eleven, an uneasy feeling gripped me. "What's going on?"

Ahmed's dark gaze didn't stray from my face. "The meeting was rescheduled." A cruel smirk lifted his thin lips.

"Then why am I here?" *What does he have up his sleeve?*

"We need to talk about your behavior. About all this

sudden interest in my business dealings. Then there's Lily." His fist slammed down on the mahogany desk, and he stood. "Whatever you've planned with my granddaughter, it will not be tolerated."

I tensed further. "I have nothing planned. Only to solidify myself in the reasons and rewards behind the missions you send me on. It's my right."

He rose then rounded the corner of his large desk, each step measured, his fury a coil waiting to spring. Yet, there would be little I could do against him. Lily's life depended on it.

"Seven minutes and twenty seconds."

"What does that even mean?" My blood chilled. I knew. It was how long Keegan and I had spoken in the alleyway.

"Jamal's men reported the unaccounted time and your disappearance from their sight."

"You're having me followed?" I feigned outrage as if it was the first time I'd realized he was watching me. "What did you seriously learn from my shopping habit?" I wanted to roll my eyes, but my tone was enough to incite his anger. "What does that say about trust, about bringing me into the fold?"

The crack of his hand on my cheek was expected, and I heard it before I felt it. I had to make it appear as if I wanted to be more a part of things, regardless of how adamant I'd been in the past to be excluded. I had to try to show support for his work. It was the only plan I had, even though it was failing dismally.

"If I must make an example of you to the public and to those in my employ, daughter, I will."

His putrid breath fanned my face. I held my ground, refusing to cower despite the throbbing along my cheek-bone. "I don't know what you're talking about. Was it while I was in my rooms? If so, how dare they spy on me in my private wing. That's my space."

"Every inch of this house is mine. Do not forget your place." His nostrils flared. "Don't think I don't notice the change in your behavior. If you attempt to cross me, others will pay for your disobedience."

That was exactly why I was getting Lily away from him. "Then what was it? When I was in the clothing store changing in the dressing room? I bought several articles of clothing. Did they report that to you? Do I not have a right to buy clothes for Lily and myself? And as to this being only your house, Lily and I are happy to leave."

Frantic pounding sounded on the closed office door, and I cursed the guards who most likely stood outside. *This is happening too soon! Please let Keegan and Lily have gotten away.*

Ahmed moved away to answer the door, his gaze burning into me until the last moment. He turned the knob, and Andrea spilled inside, wringing her hands as she looked between Ahmed and me.

"I apologize for interrupting, but I can't find Lily."

"What?" I had to appear frantic, unknowing. "She was sleeping in her room when I left."

"I know." Andrea shifted from foot to foot, her voice high and tight. "I went to check on her before I turned in to give her a kiss on the head." Fat tears rolled down her cheeks. "She wasn't there, just a pillow beneath the blanket and her doll's hair peeking from the sheets to look like her."

Pounding feet echoed through the hallway before a guard filled the doorway. I fought the urge to look at my watch. *Has enough time lapsed? Are they out of range?*

"Two guards were killed. We are searching for the intruders but have not found a breach inside."

"Alert the police," Ahmed snapped. "My granddaughter is missing. I want all the exits covered. Airport and ports."

The guard nodded before sprinting away, speaking into his communication device. I took a step to follow, but Ahmed's iron grip latched onto my arm.

"Where do you think you're going?"

"To find my daughter." I jerked free, my lips pulled back in what I hoped appeared to be feral fear spiked with cold, hard determination. "I thought you had top-notch security guarding your home. You failed. And because of that, my daughter—your granddaughter—is missing."

He would believe that I was frantic about finding my daughter or go to hell thinking about. I skirted around Andrea, whom I hadn't informed about Keegan's doings in case she slipped up and let Ahmed know something was amiss. If she'd been in her room as I'd thought she would, she too would have been taken to safety. At least she didn't know anything, accidentally damning us all.

"I'll be making a phone call," Ahmed said, effectively slowing my steps. "Hugo, Max's uncle, will know what to do to handle Max. If I find out you involved him in taking my granddaughter from me, you will wish you'd never been born, Kara," Ahmed growled after my retreating form.

I shook off his threat and resumed my pace down the hallway, but before I rounded the corner to go to my wing, I met his gaze over my shoulder. "Max is dead."

Ahmed's twisted laugh promised retribution and told me that he didn't believe what I'd said.

18

KEEGAN

IN THE EARLY-MORNING HOURS, Jack and I hid in the shadows and watched the inn where we were staying. Hired thugs and guards, who had to have been sent by Ahmed, crawled the streets nearby. By some miracle, they hadn't found us. Still, it wasn't what I expected, and a sense of impending doom hovered over me.

Before extracting Lily, we'd packed up our gear and stowed it in a new room fifteen blocks away, and farther inland. Paid handsomely, the couple who owned the inn would remain quiet for that fact alone, as the country was in political upheaval and the people were starving. The couple had friends, Janie and José, whom they promised would not report us, whose son had been killed in senseless violence in the street brought about by the government. There could be no telling anyone we were there.

An hour passed, and we remained immobile, blending into the night. We had to be sure no one had seen us. Short of waking the people who lived nearby, we'd planned for every scenario. If guards arrived to question them, we would intervene and get them to safety. For the time being, we held our position.

Before the first rays of dawn, we set out on foot to our new home away from home for the next two days. We couldn't risk staying much longer. My key objective was to get Kara out. Our mission was to recover the drones. That meant Hugo had to be found and apprehended.

Two police officers appeared out of nowhere. Jack and I had been spotted. Shouts echoed off the buildings, and we dodged into an alley. Thankfully, we didn't have Lily with us. She and Hawk were on their way out of that godforsaken place. Better we draw their notice than have them converge on us.

More men joined the others behind us. We ducked through a door hanging off its hinges and into an abandoned building. Leaping over debris, we raced to the back corner, shattered the intact window, and exited. We had a lead, but not by much. Doors crashed behind us as five men came barreling out of the building. I nudged ahead of Jack and took the next alleyway. The building three over had an entrance into tunnels below the street. That's where we could lose them. I had firsthand experience of those tunnels, as I'd used them when I'd escaped as a kid.

Jack was on my heels. Someone behind us fired shots, so we ducked and ran, dodging into alleys and behind dumpsters. The entire time, we kept moving. The streets would soon be swarmed by cops, Ahmed's guards, and possibly the Dark Wings, which I wanted to avoid. The building was ahead, and no one was behind us for the moment—we had maybe two seconds.

I busted through the door. After Jack followed, I secured it behind us. "This way." We had to get to the room where the access was hidden in a pantry. I'd learned about it by chance—it was what had saved me from detection then, and I hoped would again.

We shimmied around tables and through dimly lit rooms until we were at the door that held our escape. No sounds found us as we slipped past the doorway and into the stairwell. They hadn't seen us enter, but if they did figure it out, they would be on us in no time at all.

"How'd you know about this place?" Jack whispered beside me as we followed the tunnel down.

"This is how I got away from the Dark Wings." We were slowly jogging, splashing through a few puddles where pipes had leaked. It was musty and dark but a safe haven nonetheless. "I hid down here for days. Without it, they would have found me."

That was enough for him. He understood. Silence stretched between us as we made our way through the tunnels under the streets above where they searched for us. We had several minutes to go at least before we could go topside.

Beneath a manhole cover in the street, we waited several minutes after we heard the guards confirm the area was clear and search to the east. Cautiously, we ascended the ladder, and with my shoulder, I pushed the heavy piece of metal up enough to slide it over.

When no alarms sounded, we exited the manhole, returned the circular covering to hide our trail, then took off again at a fast pace. We'd gone out of our way and had a good distance to cover to make it to our next safe house.

My legs were tight from our flat-out sprint to get Lily free earlier, and the fifteen-block jog would do me some good, even with a heavy pack on. Soon, the city would wake. We kept to the shadows, weaving in and out of alleyways and behind brightly painted homes. Luck stayed with us, and we didn't encounter any of the many groups of criminals that ran the nights or anyone sent by Ahmed. I suspected our reprieve after the tunnels to be short-lived.

The tiny house was in sight. No lights were on inside. There would be a window toward the rear that would be unlocked, and we could enter there, free from prying eyes.

Nothing would take away the pain of the father and mother inside that home, who still grieved their son, but I hoped we could ease some of their suffering through supplies, payment, or possibly even a way out and a path to begin life elsewhere. That was something Kara and I could discuss, even though I wanted to take her away, never to return. She had been chained to others and at their beck and call, and I would never do that to her.

There was also the matter of her husband, Samir. He had what I desperately wanted: a family, and in particular, Kara and Lily. I couldn't help but wonder if their marriage was for protection rather than love.

Jack eased the window up, and while he crawled in, I kept watch. Nothing stirred. After he scoped the inside, he came back and squeezed my shoulder. I turned and faced him then hoisted myself through the square opening.

With the room secured, I dropped to the couch along the wall adjacent to the single window. The space was small, with only a narrow bed and a futon. We didn't need much, and it would do nicely.

"We need to be on the move in two hours tops," I whispered to Jack. "Depending on how Hugo and Ahmed's meeting went last night, the drones may have changed hands."

"We're running out of time." Jack leaned against the wall. "If he sold them to Ahmed, and the president gets his hands on them..."

"Right. So we'll need to make Hugo a priority." My gut was in knots and would be until I heard from Hawk that Lily was safe in Maine. Then there was Kara… At least she had the skills to take care of herself. I opened my pack, pulled out a bottle of water, and took a few sips. "I think he'll be close to where Ahmed lives. Our search should begin there. We can question the residents."

"Hopefully, they won't inform Ahmed's men about us."

Fear did strange things. "We have money. Let's offer that in exchange for information." God knows the people needed help, and we could easily spare what we had. "We need to rest. I'll take the first shift."

Jack lay back on the bed. "That's the plan, then."

In an hour, I would wake him then pass out myself. That would be enough to keep us going. If Kara got the chance, I knew she'd be in town. Maybe not right away, but even so, we had to find Hugo and put a stop to his selling the drones, if he hadn't already. We would have to split up. Jack could question the residents near Ahmed's home, and I would wait for Kara.

As I repeatedly scanned the small alleyway, the access point to where we were, Hugo's appearance came to mind. The drooping eye and beard had thrown me off, and I wondered if they were real. If so, the damage had to have been from an accident, probably a fire. No matter what had befallen him, he deserved pain and suffering. Whenever I thought of him, a red haze coated my perception, and I wasn't sure I could stop myself from killing him. Hugo was not a good person.

Nothing stirred nearby except a cool breeze. Outraged shouts and general discord were typical of the city as criminals ruled the night—Ahmed being one of sorts, himself.

I couldn't keep Hugo from my mind, even if the mission

had changed and no longer called for us to pursue him. If he didn't believe that I was dead, there would be the matter of the Dark Wings calling their due. Jamal, the leader, would welcome a chance to make me pay. In their eyes, I'd committed the ultimate sin. I'd left. And ever since my escape, I'd been marked for death.

Soon, Kara would be as well.

19

———

KARA

THE SUN WAS high in the sky, adding to the already sweltering temperature. I meandered along the city's sidewalk at a slow pace, taking time to talk with anyone I knew. It gave me time and would provide enough of a distraction for Max if he was around. I had to find him and warn him.

I clasped hands with the homeless woman, Margo, I'd been helping. Her toothless smile reflected the hollowness in her eyes. After pressing a mango and a sandwich into her arthritic hands, I secured the large purse that I'd filled with food back on my shoulder. Ahmed could go to hell for his part in starving the people. He advised the president, and he could take a stand for the people rather than lining his own pockets.

There weren't many homeless out that day, but I would feed those I could. With each step on the dusty pavement, the feel of being watched sizzled along my skin. I would not lead them to my daughter, but I had to warn Keegan. He would show, somehow. I knew it. An invisible cord seemed to connect us. I physically sensed when he was near. The heightened awareness and release of butterflies in my stomach told me that he, too, watched my progress along the street.

Every few stores, a Dark Wing soldier leaned against the building. I met their cold gazes with determination. I wouldn't let them touch me. Nor would Ahmed, at least not yet. He thought I would lead them to Lily, like a lamb to slaughter. As if.

At the end of the block, I rounded the corner and passed the abandoned pastry store, and my instincts flared. In the recessed entryway, away from the prying eyes of the soldiers, Keegan stood. We only had a couple of minutes, and while I longed to hear about Lily, I had to help him first.

I stepped on my left shoelaces and unraveled them, which gave me an excuse to bend and retie them while staying on the sidewalk and in plain sight. Under my breath, I whispered, "Ahmed knows you're alive."

"I figured. Any word on the drones?"

I dropped my right shoulder, one of the straps for my purse slid down, and I nudged a mango to roll out. Two emaciated men went down on a knee to help me. With shaky hands, the one closest picked up the fruit then passed it back to me. I wanted to cry. "No. Please, you keep it."

I pulled out two bags with a few sandwiches and several bills hidden in each. As they accepted the food I offered, I spoke in hushed tones to Keegan and implored the men with my gaze not to give away his position. "I haven't found them yet. The meeting with Hugo is rescheduled for today. An hour. I have to get back. I'll do everything I can to get what you need."

With the help of one of the too-thin men, I stood then offered each a hug to delay having to leave. We couldn't talk of my daughter, not there. There was no way I could stay, so I continued my stroll through town, away from Keegan. I had to get back to the house soon. Although Ahmed found my compassionate excursions pointless, he ignored them. I would make that meeting, no matter what.

I stumbled on the sidewalk when Keegan spoke. His rough whisper whirled through my mind, tempting me to turn back. "I need you, Kara."

———

Keegan

"I DON'T LIKE IT." I crouched before the patrol neared. Jack and I were a reasonable distance from Ahmed's home, but there was no reason to take any chances. "Using Kara to get intel on the drones is risky. Ahmed is already suspicious." Not only that, but I recognized the way she'd moved on the street earlier today. She was hurting. Our window to get her out was closing.

"I agree, but you know the ramifications of the drones falling into the president's hands. From what you told me about Kara's background and training, she can take care of herself for now."

He was right, but that didn't mean I had to like it. We'd positioned unobtrusive cameras around the property so we could monitor the comings and goings, and particularly when Hugo arrived. If he carried anything with him, we would take him before he entered the residence. If not, we had to count on Kara to intercept what was happening.

On our phones, we could keep several main angles on display then toggle through some of the lesser possible entry points as needed. I swiped a hand over my tired eyes in an attempt to clear my vision. Due to Lily's disappearance the night before, the meeting with Hugo would be heavily guarded. Or at least that's what we assumed. I didn't get a chance to confirm with Kara.

I zoomed in on camera six as the guards made rounds in that section of the yard. "They added more security. I recognize two from the Dark Wings." I didn't want Jack involved.

"Stop worrying."

"I didn't say anything."

Jack rolled his shoulders. "Didn't need to. It's written all over your face. I know how you fight, which gives me an advantage they won't be expecting. I can hold my own well enough with them."

"Stay away from Jamal. If he shows, I don't want you or Kara engaging."

Silence stretched between us, heavy and expectant. He was going to push for answers. I'd given him and Hawk a good portion of what had happened and who these people were, but it wasn't enough, and I couldn't expect him to wade into war without the history and battle plan.

"What happened between you and your uncle? Why is leaving the outfit still a problem for you?"

Baring my soul wasn't something that came naturally, but I would do it if even a shred of understanding could keep Jack safe. "My parents were affiliated with the Dark Wings, as is Hugo. They wanted out and were killed because of it. My guess is by Hugo's hand."

"I can see why you hate him."

"There's more." Not only didn't I want them to know about my relation to Hugo, but during my time in the Dark Wings, I'd done terrible things in order to survive. "Once they were dead, Hugo decided he'd be the one to initiate me. It wasn't pleasant: the training, the abuse, the fear, killing for them. I was eleven when I was dumped in the mercenary group and put under Jamal's instruction. There were rules we could not break. For me, there were two major ones. To leave the outfit meant death. And upon my sixteenth birthday, Hugo would return, and I'd fall under his command, killing the targets he deemed necessary."

Jack's features hardened. "Are you and Jamal matched fighters?"

"If I'd stayed, I would have surpassed him. They had ways of keeping us in line."

Jack frowned. "The scars on your back?"

That day flashed in my mind with the velocity of a train wreck.

Kara had failed to kill her target, something I'd been tasked to make sure she was ready for.

The crack of the whip hissed through the air and burned across my back, tearing flesh in its wake. Drops of blood decorated the ground. I bit down on a piece of leather, straining against the ropes that bound my arms. I focused on Kara's muffled cries, not the jeers from the men who surrounded me.

I cared for her. It could lead to my downfall, possibly to hers. They would not know.

Jamal's dusty boots were within my line of sight as he ordered five more lashes. I refused to look at him. The scar that marred his face from cheekbone to chin had been my doing two years before. Even at thirteen, they'd molded me into a feral animal, a force that few could contain.

Kara had messed up, badly. Allowed to go on a mission with myself and another, she'd faltered and hadn't made the kill. An alarm had gone up before I could get to him and slit his throat. Hesitation killed, and Jamal didn't train his soldiers to harbor compassion or indecision.

Her mistake would require punishment. I was her trainer. He thought punishing me would resolve the problem, effectively trickling down to her. Her father, Ahmed, probably wouldn't have allowed marks upon her skin. That had been the only thing that'd saved her from the whip.

I shook my head, pulling myself out of the past. We had a job to do, and it needed to end that day if not the next, at the latest. Each day that passed decreased our odds of recovering the drones and getting Kara out. Jack nudged me, stirring to mind the question he'd asked about the scars.

"Yes, but the punishment was worth it." She was worth it.

20
___

KEEGAN

Hugo never showed for the meeting the day after Lily was rescued, which was cause for alarm. Ahmed had strung Kara along about Hugo's presence at one meeting or another. The stakes were so high that it seemed Hugo had fled the country with Ahmed's help. The more time that passed without a sighting indicated a good chance that Hugo was gone. Then there was the other possibility we couldn't dismiss. If the drones were transferred to the Venezuelan president, we would have to infiltrate his home.

The roar of the protesting crowd from the front of Ahmed's house echoed through the streets in muffled waves.

"We have to check in with the guys, and we can't do it here." Jack holstered his gun under his shirt.

I did the same. There was little chance anything would happen before dark with the protesters out front again. As we made our way back to our base, I couldn't stop my mind from imagining different scenarios between Ahmed and Kara. The various possibilities of how she might suffer for

Lily's extraction ate at me. I should have insisted that she come, too, stormed Ahmed's office, and taken her out of there. It wasn't the best way to handle things, but it would have gone a long way to alleviate the ulcer I was surely developing.

Back in the cramped room, Jack called Rich. As soon as he answered, Jack put him on speaker so we could both talk.

Rich's baritone burst from the speaker. "We have news back from the medical examiner, and it's not good, gentlemen. The director of National Intelligence Services, who fell ill at the last meeting, was poisoned with the organophosphorus compound VX."

Jack and I exchanged uneasy glances. The extremely lethal and odorless chemical would block enzymes affecting the glands and organs, which resulted in heart failure.

"Were you able to get a signature on the nanoweapon used?" I knew it would come up as GH Envirotech, but with Rich's confirmation, we would have access to whatever we needed to apprehend the remaining drones and those in possession of them.

"We were. It was GH Envirotech, George Hammond's company. Following the identification of the poison, we seized their office computers." We heard movement in the room as Rich put us on speaker. "I also have Liam and Mike here."

Good. We needed to touch base with our team, and their presence must have meant the interrogation was complete. "What did you learn about the US half of the business? Is George guilty?" If he was, he could have a wealth of information that would be useful in helping us find where the missing drones were.

Mike's gruff voice crackled over the line. "George held

out on us about the drones made here. But they were different than what was produced in the Caracas plant. The ones here were for farmers."

"The US plant was developing pollinating insects for crops." Liam's Irish accent complemented Mike's harsher vowels. "We questioned him thoroughly, and aside from the larger drone that would fly overhead, connecting to the smaller wireless units, he was unaware the Caracas branch was developing anything different."

"What did he think they were doing?" Jack drummed his fingers on the windowsill in our room.

"He thought they would offer the drones to the people of Caracas to help with the food shortages." Mike filled us in. "The partner in Caracas who died of a heart attack was getting ready to pull out before the company was seized. He'd sent two emails to George that Chris was able to retrieve. In one, he shared doubts about Henry Adams. It seemed he was utilizing a few from their team to work on another project that hadn't gotten approval. And when questioned, Henry wasn't forthcoming."

"You said two emails."

"Yeah, the second one was just located, and Chris unraveled the encryption. It seems the Venezuelan partner did some snooping and discovered there were six prototypes that Henry was working on. He couldn't find any evidence of others made, or the designs. That's the last contact. George didn't know what type of drones or their purpose. He also found out his partner died minutes after the email was sent."

"The prototypes are the nanoweapons we're after." That made sense, but it also told us we'd hit a dead end. Hugo, known to George as Henry Adams, would be the only one with details. There wouldn't be a paper trail anywhere, nor would the other employees be privy to his scheme.

"That isn't all." Mike's crisp voice honed my attention. "Chris got a hit on Hugo clearing customs to the US. Our best guess is he's here to complete the objective of wiping out Venezuela's opposition in the upcoming National Security Council meeting."

Rich had high-level clearance about the meeting's agenda and what would be determined. In several days, the members of National Security Council would determine the threat level of the Venezuelan president and if an assassination would be the ultimate course of action.

"We need you home, gentlemen," Rich commanded.

After ending the call, I ground my teeth. I wanted that fucker dead, but I had an even bigger priority. "I'm not going. Not until I get Kara out."

"I don't want to leave you here without backup." Jack moved to gather the few things we'd scattered around the room, shoving them into his pack.

"I won't be long, and Kara will be my backup on the way out. Just make sure the boat is returned after you cross the Caribbean Sea."

Jack stopped what he was doing and took in my stance. I'd widened my legs and crossed my arms over my chest. I knew he would understand. If he'd had a chance when we were in high school, I knew he would have done things differently where his girlfriend, Jenny, was concerned. I had my chance.

"Keep us posted," he said, "and I want you out in two days, no matter what. We'll need you to secure the National Security Council members and neutralize the threat if it hasn't been done prior."

I nodded. After I saw him off, I would concentrate on

Kara. If she learned that Ahmed had any additional prototypes, I would be there to follow that lead. It was doubtful. Our best guess was that the drones remained with Hugo.

We had to stop Ahmed and Hugo before a swarm of insect robots wiped out members of our government.

21

KARA

NIGHTTIME WAS the worst time to be out on the streets in Caracas. Anyone who dared took precautions by carrying weapons. I hated what had happened to the city. I should have thought of it as mine, but in a way, it had never been home to me. It was just another jail.

Keegan will find me. I wasn't the type of woman who relied on others, but I needed help to ensure Lily got away if there was any chance of escape. There were too many eyes on her whereabouts at all times, especially if we left the grounds together. Keegan had always been a hero to me, and in that lockbox within my heart, I prayed he would continue to be, so I could reunite with my daughter.

He'd flashed his cell when we'd had one of those rare stolen moments on the sidewalk. On the screen were dozens of views from the cameras he had stationed around Ahmed's home. I had every faith he would see that I snuck out and find me. There were things we needed to discuss.

Belting the sweater wrap tight around my waist to ward off the chilly air, I slipped between the foliage. I'd recognized the angle of one of the cameras as being one I could easily reach. Scanning the branches with a small penlight, two trees later, I found it. Clicking the light on and off twice, I sent him a message. I stood there a moment longer on the off chance he was close.

As the seconds ticked by, I knew I couldn't wait. I took off in the direction of the building he and I had squatted in when the kidnappers had chased us with guns. There wouldn't be anyone there, and the safest place for us was within the thick den of thieves and criminals.

With sure steps, I raced through the streets to where I kept a Ducati. A trusted family stored it for me, and I paid them monthly for the privilege. I had to have a way to get away from Ahmed. I wound my hair into a tight bun at the base of my neck then opened the trunk that held my gear. My heart squeezed painfully at the sight of the tiny helmet nestled beside mine. It was for Lily if we needed to escape at a moment's notice. *Please be safe, baby*. I missed her desperately.

With the helmet securely on and hiding my features, I added a leather jacket that none within Ahmed's household would recognize as mine. I wheeled the bike out, threw my leg over, started it up, and took off down the street, kicking it into high gear after the first block. No need to wake anyone amidst the sleepy subdivision.

Eyes constantly scanning the streets and sidewalks, I stayed wary of an attack. Kidnappers were out in force at night, as were common street thugs who would rob anyone of anything they had. I didn't need the hassle. My heart wept with fear that my daughter hadn't gotten to Samir or that she was scared, even hurt.

The abandoned building loomed ahead. Windows partially boarded the front, and no lights were on. I cut the engine on my bike after turning into the alley beside the structure. We'd blown up a portion of the sidewall, and a gaping hole provided the perfect entrance to push my motorcycle through. Once inside, I dismounted. I was early. *Please be here soon, Keegan.*

"So, this is to be our meeting place?"

I whirled around, heart in my throat. He rose to his full height from the far corner behind me, looming in that way he did. Barely leashed energy crackled around him, filling the chaotic wreckage inside with the immediate sense of expectancy, of action. He was a force, one I'd been drawn to since I was a mere kid.

All the emotions I'd kept locked down strained, breaking the chains until a tear trickled down my cheek. Then I was in motion. Running. Leaping. His arms wrapped around me, and I clung to him, my face buried against his neck.

In his arms, I absorbed some of his strength and let him shoulder the weight I'd carried since before Kara was born. God, I was so scared of his answer, but I had to ask, "Is she safe?"

He held the back of my head with one of his large hands, cradling me to him. A shiver ran through my body, but the overwhelming uncertainty of what would happen still had me in its grip.

"She arrived a little over an hour ago and is being guarded by my family."

"What?" My head snapped back, and I looked at him with horror. "Hugo?"

"No, never him. My military family. The women there will spoil her rotten. You have nothing to worry about." With the pad of his finger, he swept away the river of tears.

"And Samir?" I wanted her to have someone familiar

there with her. The look that came over his face was down-right volatile. "What is it?"

"He isn't her father, is he, Kara?"

He knows. "He is in the way that matters."

"That isn't what I was asking."

I wanted to lie my head on his chest and not have the conversation. But I couldn't, especially with the potential of his fury about not being told detonating. Still... "What does it matter? She's mine. I won't let anyone take her from me."

"I would never do that, Kara." His voice gentled. "Just tell me. Am I her biological father?"

My stomach cramped, and an onslaught of new tears fell from my eyes. I swiped them away, angered by my weakness. "Yes."

He crushed me to him, and I felt the tremor that ran through his body. Seconds then a few minutes passed before he eased away, and he unwound his arms. Setting me on my feet, he took my hands in his. "Why didn't you tell me? You would have been able to find me based on what I told you that night."

I scrubbed at my face with my hands and put a stop to the tears, to the momentary weakness he'd witnessed. "I knew you that night as Max, despite you telling me you went by Keegan. You had a life free from the Dark Wings. While I could have found you had I tried, I couldn't risk it. Nor could I do that to you after you'd escaped and remained off their radar. Ahmed was already suspicious of whose baby I carried, and then there was Jamal. They work together, and I feared for both you and Lily if they'd known you were her father."

"Ahmed believes Samir is?"

"Ahmed has his suspicions. Samir is gay, but that isn't widely known. When I came back after you and I'd spent the night together, Samir was single. After I found out I was pregnant, we fabricated our story that the baby was his." I shrugged. I stood by my decision. "Samir is my best friend. He would have done anything for me. And he did."

"Drunk or not, if he's gay, there wouldn't be anything happening between you two."

"We said he found women equally attractive, and he's always been a trusted friend of mine. It didn't hurt that his eye color was somewhat close to yours." Samir's were more brown than green, but it was enough. "He agreed to marry me, and if my daughter was born with green eyes, it wouldn't have been a stretch."

"Why would he do this for you? What's in it for him?" A muscle ticked by the side of his jaw.

"You mean, can I trust him?" My back snapped straight. "You left. I did the best I could here, and I think I did a pretty damn good job of keeping my baby safe. Samir may have gained security from being married to me, but not in the way you're thinking. He is loyal to Lily and me."

"I don't know him, and because of that, he will not take Lily from the house."

"What house? And that's not fair. Lily needs him. To her, Samir is her father."

"Samir will be contacted in a few hours and brought in to see her. He can stay should he choose to. But Lily will not leave without you, and that is non-negotiable."

It took me a second to process that he was telling me to push past the fear of losing my daughter to her biological father. But that wasn't what he was doing. He wasn't trying to take her from me, to bar her from the only father she'd known. Instead, he wanted her guarded, safe until I could go to her. "Okay." I trusted Keegan with my life after all he'd done for me, and I would trust him with Lily's too.

His eyes bore into mine in that way of his, as if he was seeing inside me, my every thought and intent bare to him. There was no need for walls. I let him see the truth to my words. I did trust him. The relief crashing through me in waves ever since he told me Lily was safe was enough for me.

"Do you know if Ahmed has the drones?" he asked quietly.

I shook my head. "The only thing I was able to find out from hacking into his bank accounts is that he transferred a huge sum of money from one account." I handed Keegan the piece of paper with the account information written on it. "Jamal has been at the house daily, and they've been locked in Ahmed's office. Whatever is going to go down must be happening soon."

"It is. We have a few days tops, then our chance of recovery will be gone. If you are able, find anything that points to the meetings with the president or Hugo. Anything that indicates it's significant. We think he's launching a political attack within the US, but..." He hesitated.

"Ahmed doesn't only go after politicians in his or the president's way," I said. "I can tell you that his interests are purely selfish. That means if he's trying to get in bed with another company and if there is resistance, accidents or death will follow."

"Then you know what to look for. Also, check for when he's meeting with the president. We fear he has already made the transaction to get a portion of the nanoweapons into his hands. I need to get into the house and search for the drones. Or is there any other place Ahmed keeps records or weapons?"

"I don't know of any, but that doesn't mean there isn't." I hated admitting that to him. While we were in the training camp, Keegan didn't know everything behind why I was there. Ahmed portrayed me as a pampered princess, saying he wanted me to be highly trained for my own protection due to his unstable position. Keegan had his own problems, and I don't think he recognized the extent of Ahmed's hatred for me. He played the game exceptionally well, always wearing a façade in public of the doting father. In truth, he was anything but.

Keegan shifted and was suddenly closer. My fingers trembled, and I curled them into my palms, fighting against the need to touch him. *What would he do if I reached out, pulled him close?*

Our gazes met and held. Electricity crackled between us. Then he cupped the back of my neck, closed the distance between us, and covered my mouth with his. Sparks of light exploded behind my closed eyelids as I let myself feel passion for the first time in five years. He took his time exploring my mouth, and when he broke our kiss, I would have stumbled if it hadn't been for his arm around my waist, holding me up. His forehead rested against mine as we fought to regain our breath.

"Your marriage—"

"Is in name only." I could tell him. He would never betray me. "Samir and I have talked about what could be, if we ever got away from my father." I'd opened up more than I should have. Time was running out, and I had to get back in the store. "I've got to go. I'll do everything I can to get the drones or whatever my father has that could help you."

Keegan was silent, probably putting two and two together. "Do what you can. After tomorrow night, Kara, I want you out of there. I'll be coming for you."

My pulse skyrocketed. No woman's heart would be safe after hearing those words from someone like him.

22

———

KARA

With my elbows on the vanity, I rested my head against my palms and breathed. *I can do this.* Not much scared me except harm coming to Lily. *She's safe.* That was what I had to focus on. That and helping to find the information Keegan required so I could get out of there. Once in the States, we would be free, at least sort of.

Keegan's help eased my mind in more ways than he would ever know. But if he could figure out how to get both of us out without fulfilling the exit requirement from the Dark Wings... I didn't know if it would be possible, short of staging my death. Or maybe I was exempt. Maybe the connection was Ahmed, and I was only the tool.

They didn't let anyone go. Keegan had been an exception, a mistake on their part. He'd become a chameleon, a ghost, one they hadn't been able to find. *Would we be lucky twice?*

The more I thought about our situation, the greater the risks appeared. Jamal had to die along with any ties we had to him.

I lifted my head and stared into the mirror above the

sink. Dark, haunted eyes with half-moons clinging beneath them gazed back at me. They wouldn't need to be covered up. With my haggard appearance, Ahmed might believe I'd lost sleep due to fear over Lily's safety and not because of the man who'd birthed the method of her escape.

The bristles of the brush scraped my scalp as I worked the knots from my hair then secured the long strands in a high ponytail. Dressed in black, I planned to blend in with the shadows while searching for Keegan's drones.

It was before dawn, and that time between two and three in the morning when most of the household was in a deep sleep was the perfect time to search Ahmed's office and possibly his bedroom.

I let myself out of the bathroom and crept through my bedroom then into the hall. Andrea's door was shut, the light off. I didn't want to wake her. In time, I would confide some of what was going on, enough to give her the option to leave with me if she chose. I thought she might be able to help locate the drones. Sometimes, Andrea heard things as she moved through the house—she was invisible to people like Ahmed.

His agenda was all that had ever mattered. After Lily was born, I'd stayed home for the first few months before Ahmed sent me out on missions again. The time with her had been a gift, one he'd made sure to drill home daily during that time.

With a turn of the doorknob and a gentle push, I exited the suite of rooms I shared with Lily and Andrea. The hum of the air conditioner filled the silence as I moved through the halls, turning down the ones that would take me to Ahmed's office. I loved that time of the morning. Virtually everyone was asleep.

Silvery moonlight lit my way as it spilled through the

large window at the end of the corridor. With my back flat to the wall, I held still inches from Ahmed's door, listening for any movement inside. No light shone from beneath the door, but I wasn't willing to take chances.

I pulled the tools I needed to pick the lock from my pocket, took a knee, and got to work. Breaking in was easy, something I was taught well to do, especially given the needs Ahmed had to obtain information about his business acquisitions. Working for the Venezuelan president wasn't his only endeavor.

The tumblers clicked into place. With a simple turn of the lock, the obstacle was gone. I grasped the handle, twisted it, and eased the door open a crack. Darkness met my limited view. I withdrew my penlight then shone it along the slit, checking for any hidden wires. There had never been any before, as he was overconfident and thought himself untouchable, but Ahmed's trust in me was at an all-time low, and I had to be sure.

The door clicked shut behind me, throwing the room into pitch black. I didn't dare turn on a light. The penlight would have to do. The top of his desk was neat and orderly with nothing out of place. I was more interested in the contents within, anyway, and the safe. I started with the desk and got to work unlocking the drawers before riffling through each one.

I slipped a thumb drive from my back pocket and inserted it and one of the USB drives from the handfuls in the drawer to the right into the laptop on his desk. I began the process of copying the files, but I would have to look over the contents later. I doubted there would be anything of use, but it was better safe than sorry. With the lack of tiny drones or references to them in his desk, I prepared to crack his safe.

Behind the desk was a large oil painting that hid his safe —not very original. Time was passing quicker than I would have liked. Fortunately, the lock was old-school rather than electronic. In the silence, it was easy to listen for the tiny metallic clicks when the correct number registered. Turning the knob to the right twice in minuscule increments, I stopped at the nine when the slight sound pinged. Two more numbers, then the release popped.

Please be here. I swung open the safe and shone my light inside. Stacks of money took up an entire shelf. On the top one sat another USB drive and several documents. My nerves stretched thin. I'd been in there too long. Riffling through the papers, I didn't see anything regarding the drones. They were mostly business documents, passports, and a letter. My focus had to be the electronic files. I plugged the stick into his laptop and downloaded the contents onto my portable drive while putting everything else exactly as it had been in the safe.

That's when I saw it, a small mosquito, barely visible in the back of the safe. With care, I lifted it by one of its wings. I feared I would break it if I shoved it into my pocket. Rifling through Ahmed's drawers, I found a permanent marker. I took the cap off the pen then dropped the mini drone inside before slipping it into my pocket. My heart pounded. It was what Keegan wanted. So did Ahmed. There was no doubt at that point about my precarious position under his roof.

A few more seconds passed, and then the red light stopped flashing on the drive, indicating the process was complete. I disconnected the flash drive from the port, put it back, then shut the safe and returned the painting to its rightful place. Then I shoved the slim high-capacity drive inside my bra to conceal it and got the hell out of there. I'd spent forty-five minutes in Ahmed's office and was damn lucky no one discovered me.

I rounded the corner and was almost to my wing when I saw him. Ice shot through my veins, and my hands tingled from the shock. One of Jamal's mercenaries stood outside my door. If they found the drive on me, it would be game over—I would be worse than dead.

23

———

KARA

My back slammed against the wall. Andrea cried out from within my rooms.

"Get your hands off me." I blocked Jamal's soldier from curling his fingers in my shirt. "You have no grounds here." I waved him away. "Go now, before I report what you've done." *How did they know I left my wing?*

"Where were you?" His expression blank, he crowded me back.

"None of your business. I don't answer to you." Off to one side, Andrea wrung her hands. Something had to be done quickly.

A cruel smile curved his thin lips. "Today, you do. I have orders to monitor your activities. Wandering around at this time is suspicious. Jamal will want to talk to you. Come."

"I'm not going anywhere with you." *No way.* "Listen, every minute you waste your time focusing on me, you aren't finding my daughter. If she has a single scratch on her, I will personally carve you, her grandfather, and Jamal into tiny pieces." I knocked his shoulder out of the way and entered my suite, the drone and thumb drive in my possession making me more than aware of my precarious position. Thankfully, he didn't bar me from going in. *Interesting.*

I shut and locked the door behind me then grabbed Andrea by the arm and pulled her away from the door in case it was kicked in. I didn't think it would be. He would've tried to stop me from entering in the first place. Maybe he didn't have orders, but was just being a dick.

I wondered who was watching me, Ahmed or Jamal. My guess was that Jamal was acting on his own and either hadn't given explicit instructions to his guard dog or hadn't had the time to be specific. Regardless, they were monitoring everything I did. *I can't stay here.* It was time to go.

My adrenaline escalated at the thought. But first, I had to calm Andrea, find out what happened, and figure out if she was leaving with me.

I rubbed her arms then pulled her to me and squeezed her tightly. "Everything's okay. Did he come in here? Threaten you?"

"No." She sniffed, and I released her from my embrace. She wiped the moisture from under her eyes. "I woke from pounding on the door. I hoped it was news of Lily, but it was that man, demanding to know where you were."

"I couldn't sleep. Rather than pacing in here and waking you, I walked around the house." The less she knew, the better for her safety. "Are you sure you're all right?"

She nodded. "Yes. I'm just so worried about Lily. I don't understand who could have taken her. How?"

"We'll find out." I infused steel in my voice. More than anything, I wanted to tell her, but I had a strong suspicion there were listening devices in my suite. They suspected I was involved in her disappearance, but torturing me for the details wouldn't serve their purpose, at least not yet. However, that could come sooner than I thought. Even though I wanted to confide in Andrea—she'd been by my side when I'd had Lily and a constant source of comfort even before that—I couldn't.

And she'd known my mother. I trusted her.

"I feel partly responsible." Andrea shifted from foot to foot. "Your mother trusted me to keep you safe, and she would have done anything for Lily."

I smiled sadly. "I miss her." Mom had always been my first line of defense. "She would have raised hell."

"Sweetheart"—Andrea lifted my ponytail and smoothed the long strands over my shoulder—"you are just like her. She'd be so proud." She sniffled then swiped at a tear. "I am too. And I also miss her, but you have Mr. Hernandez, and he will always do right by you and Lily."

No, he would not. But she had a different view as my mom's good friend, and she saw only the best in her best friend's husband, who'd given her a job to help me with Lily when she was down on her luck. I didn't think she would ever understand or see the bad side to Ahmed, even when it was right in her face.

I squeezed her arm, not quite ready to impart my secrets to her. If Jamal or his men got to her, and they would, she would fold. "Let's get some sleep, and we can talk about it in the morning."

Andrea nodded then went back to her room. The door closed behind her with a quiet click. I remained there for a few more seconds, listening. There was no doubt in my mind I'd been overheard. I'd stood near enough to the door that they could have heard every word.

There wasn't much time. On silent feet, I padded to my room and shut the door behind me. I wouldn't be able to take the drive. I stripped out of my shirt and bra then grabbed the lace undergarment I'd sewn hidden pockets in. There were several concealed compartments for tiny flash drives sitting inside the pushup support. I secured the miniature drone in one of them. On the off chance they stopped me and patted me down, they wouldn't find what I was hiding.

I transferred the saved files onto several thumbnail-sized drives then searched for the things I couldn't leave behind. Thankfully, I'd already sent what I could through the mail to Samir during one of my many trips to town. I'd started that upon overhearing Ahmed reference the good fortune of Samir working with David's company, Meyer Ancestry Labs. Plans were in motion to do something to David, but I didn't know what, nor had I figured out the exact danger to Samir, only that it existed.

I made my peace with leaving. I wanted weapons but couldn't justify more than a knife in one of the pockets of my black cargo pants, at my thigh, and one strapped at my ankle. If I took a gun, they'd know for sure, and it wasn't worth the risk. I typically wore the knives, so it was nothing out of the ordinary.

Once the files had downloaded, I wiped the drive clean and tossed it into my desk. The tiny flash drives went into the hidden pockets in my bra. I got dressed then lay down to think.

What am I going to do about Andrea? Tears misted my eyes, and I blinked them back. Ahmed treated her well. He wouldn't hold her responsible. If I tried to bring her with me, the chance of her being caught and tortured or killed was too high. Escaping on my own should keep her safe, or at least alive.

I had to leave alone. The sooner, the better. They were

watching my rooms, so there would be no way I could exit from my suite, or even out the window. I had to think of another way.

There was one. Rolling to my feet, I got what I needed from my desk then went into the hall, closing my bedroom door behind me as if I was still within.

My lockpicking tools were in my jeans, including the miniature screwdrivers. There was an air duct in the hallway that was large enough for me to crawl into. As quickly as I could, I unscrewed the vent and removed it, swapping the screws for longer, thinner ones. The grate rested against the wall as I backed in. I shimmied far enough so that I could still reach the metal covering.

Lifting it, I aligned the screws and threaded them through. Once in place, I clamped on small metal clips I'd pocketed to make it appear as if nothing had been tampered with. The covering would hold and give the appearance that nothing was amiss. It would buy me some time. I hoped.

I'd been in there before and knew my way out. The cold from the metal seeped into my palms and knees as I moved through the ducts. I breathed through my mouth to avoid getting dust into my nose—a sneeze would draw attention. It wasn't the most comfortable option, but I could manage, and it would get me to the wing they wouldn't expect me to leave from, the south one, close to where Ahmed slept.

Please, Keegan, look at the monitors.

––––––––

Keegan

My gut told me something would go down today with Kara's search for the nanoweapons. The threat of the Dark Wings over our heads was too high a risk for me to ignore. I couldn't leave her to fend for herself. If they caught her, I didn't even want to imagine what they would do to her. I knew one thing for certain: she would wish for death before they were done.

Because I had.

The first rays of the sun cast a deceptive glow on Caracas, making the city look peaceful despite the turmoil and starvation. I'd heard people say that the country was no longer the one they'd known in their youth, but to me, there wasn't much difference from when I'd been there before. Growing up and surviving where and how I had left only bad memories with a smattering of good ones—the ones that featured my time with Kara or before my parents were killed.

Jack had left, and Chris was following up on the lead about the account Kara had disclosed. We would learn soon what was there. I'd given her a small window of time to search Ahmed's home for the drones or any evidence she could gather. I wondered whether Ahmed's large bank transfer was to Hugo—not only that, but whether the money was payment to initiate and fulfill a terrorist act against the United States' government. The account the funds were transferred into should give us some indication one way or the other. My gut said it was one of Hugo's.

An hour into my walk, I found a spot on the side of a building that would provide the coverage I needed. Ball cap pulled low, I leaned my shoulder against the wall, hidden well enough by the shadows.

With my phone in my hand, I kept an eye on the monitors. Something told me Kara would be coming out hot, and

I needed to be there to intercept any conflict. More than any other time, I committed to righting the wrongs of leaving her behind. I'd seen an opportunity to leave and had taken it without a second thought. Had I known what her life with Ahmed would become, I would've helped her escape from Jamal's camp when we were teenagers. We could both have lived in the warehouse with Jack, Mike, Hawk, and the rest of the crew. It was something I would always regret.

Connecting with her again felt like fate, had I believed in such things. Our paths crossed for the third time. Every time I was near her, I wanted to take her in my arms, kiss her senseless, make her mine. If Ahmed or the Dark Wings even thought to kill her and take her from me, I would rip their goddamn hearts out of their chests and shove them down their throats.

I blinked to clear my mind of the bloodbath I would rain down on them when a movement on camera six drew my focus. I clicked on the frame, and the picture filled my phone's screen. *Shit.* She was coming out of an upstairs window on the south side of the manor. There wasn't anything for her to climb down except for the drainpipe, and the chances of that holding her were slim.

It would take me fifteen minutes to get there in a flat-out sprint. I contemplated getting the motorcycle she had stashed, but it was too far away. I would have to run or thumb a ride.

There were guards all over the place. As I sprinted, I added another of the camera angles of the front of the house to monitor. Protesters were out in full swing, probably because of the broadcast last night. The news highlights on my phone had shown images of the president along with his advisors and friends—Ahmed was one of them—dining on an abundance of gourmet food and wine. In the next panel, pictures of stores with nearly empty shelves, looting, and poverty illustrated the vast differences between the people and their leadership. The food crisis had escalated to horrifying levels.

The protestors would surely see Kara climbing down from a side window, but I didn't know whether they would turn her in—I had to believe they wouldn't. She wasn't part of the corruption. Instead, she offered solutions, handing out food and money when she went into town. I kicked my sprint into overdrive as the first flaming bottle was thrown over the fence. *Please let this be a distraction for her benefit.*

Every block, I checked the cameras. She was clear of the house and maneuvering behind the soldiers. The mob seemed to be in even more of a frenzy. A curtain shifted, and a face appeared—spotting Kara on the lawn. The front door swung open. A woman launched herself from the entryway, her arms waving in Kara's direction as she called to her. *No...*

That was all it took for a soldier to look behind him, spot Andrea, then follow her path. My breath sawed in and out. I was so close, but all I could do was watch in horror as Kara turned. The guard broke off from the others.

The top of the manor was in sight. People were emerging from their homes, the noise of the protest reaching deafening heights. *Please let me get to her in time.* The cutout in the fence would still be there, but she wasn't near that area. Without gloves to get past the barbed wire, I had to wing it.

Pushing off my back leg, I launched myself at the fence. My hands curled around the vertical metal rod between two of the fences. In a push-pull manner, I scaled the pole. With my hands cupping the top of the beam, I heaved myself up and over, tucking my legs up and to the side to clear the barbed wire, then dropped about ten feet. I felt the impact from my feet up through my shins when I landed in a crouch.

Trees and bushes obscured my view, forming a natural barrier from the unappealing fence at my back. Gun in hand, I parted the branches and pushed through. Mass chaos greeted me. The guards were mostly busy with the protesters. Glass bottles exploded. One guard went down, screaming as fire licked his pant leg.

Two soldiers engaged with Kara. No—they were not soldiers but Dark Wing mercenaries. I didn't recognize them except that they wore all black, lacking the insignia on their shirt the other guards wore.

Kara was holding her own, but barely. A blow to the head had her staggering and down on a knee. I roared. My feet left the ground as I leapt into the air, putting the momentum behind the power of my punch. The man turned as my fist connected with his face.

The satisfying crunch of bone splintering beneath my fist didn't slow me down. Kara regained her feet, relief stark on her face.

She flung her hand out in the direction from which I'd come. Then, to the nanny, she screamed, "Run!"

Andrea took off toward the fence, leaving Kara and me to take down the two guards. My guy was up. He spun and thrust his leg at my gut. I pulled my knife out and dodged the hit by a millimeter. *My turn.*

The soldier threw a combination punch. I blocked it then struck back. The blade sank into his kidney. I shifted for a counter. His fist slammed into my jaw, and he was on me like a fucking monkey.

We don't have time for this. When an opening presented itself after several more exchanges, I sliced my knife across his neck. My guy was down. Kara's was wavering. More men were on their way. I couldn't risk Jamal's attack—he would slow us down to the point of capture. I snaked my arm around Kara, jerked her to me, withdrew my gun, then fired. Her attacker dropped, and then we were running. It would be close.

As one, we burst through the shrubs. The guards who had seen the fight break out weren't far behind. Andrea stood next to the fence, waiting. She wasn't much older than Kara, but I doubted she could scale the fence. *Fuck. She'll slow us down.*

"Is this the best idea?"

Kara met my gaze with determination. "Yes."

I dropped my pack at her feet, my gun still secure in my hand. "Bolt cutters are inside."

That's all she needed. As she unzipped the bag and retrieved what she wanted, I turned to the guards that were on us. There was no need to kill them all. The men weren't a threat like the Dark Wing soldiers were. The guards didn't raise their weapons until they got sight of me. Kara must still have been under Ahmed's protection. Good.

I fired off five shots in rapid succession, alternating the target between the most pressing threats: left, right, straight, then right. I hit the shoulders of each one's dominant hand. Guns clattered to the ground. More men advanced. We had to leave. More Dark Wings would hunt us soon.

Kara shoved Andrea through the fence. After another round then a new clip, I followed. My pack was over Kara's shoulders, its heavy weight slapping her as she ran. Andrea was a hindrance. She wasn't fast, and she was arguing with Kara.

"We must go back," Andrea pleaded, her breath labored.

"No," Kara snapped. "You don't have to go, but I do. There's nothing here for me anymore."

"Lily!" Andrea cried.

"I'm going to her." Kara's voice gentled. "Are you in?"

Determination settled over Andrea's overexerted features. "Yes."

Christ. This is the worst timing for them to have a heart-to-heart. Kara led, and I covered our backs. We turned right at the first block, heading back toward the town and away from the ocean. Shouts rang out behind us, then the screech of tires.

"We need a vehicle!" I shouted over the sound of rubber squealing around the corner.

"This way!" Kara veered left. We raced across the street and between two homes.

Andrea stopped, and Kara half turned. When Andrea pulled a phone from her pocket, Kara's eyes went wide. Guilt flashed over Andrea's features, and she thumbed her screen to the left, pulling up an app. As she depressed something on the screen, I lunged to grab the phone. Kara screamed and went down. *What the hell happened?*

My fingers curled around the phone. Wrenching it from her hand, I moved to Kara and dropped to the ground. Her eyes were half-mast. She moaned. My heart thudded against my ribs as I scanned every inch of her. *Where is she hit?*

That's when I saw the app on Andrea's phone. Whatever it was had triggered something for Kara, maybe a drug. "What did you do to her?!" My hand wrapped around Andrea's neck, and I slammed her against the side of the building.

"I followed orders." The corners of her mouth rose into a sneer. "You shouldn't have tried to leave," she said to Kara.

"What the fuck was injected into her?" There had to be a capsule under her skin somewhere that had been triggered by the app. I dropped the phone and smashed it with my heel. With my gun against Andrea's temple, I pressed my forearm against her throat, not enough to cut off her air supply but to cause her to panic. Kara lay still on the ground, and I wanted to cut Andrea.

"Don't know." Her hands gripped my arm, nails digging in.

"How long until it kills her?" It couldn't have been harmless. Jamal wouldn't mess around, and this had him and Ahmed written all over it.

"Not sure. Where's Lily?"

"I don't know." *Fuck her.* I clipped her with the butt of my gun, and she fell in a crumpled heap to the ground.

Thankfully, the guards hadn't seen us go between the houses. I had a few more seconds. I had to get Kara somewhere safe and figure out what was in her system.

Making quick work of disabling Andrea's phone, I peered around the corner of the house we were squatting against to see what was happening in the streets. Three soldiers had their backs to us, moving slowly, checking the area. We didn't have much time before more came. We needed to find somewhere to lie low.

Kara lay there, her body deadly still. A fine sheen of sweat covered her face. I pulled the pack off her and slipped it on my back. "Where's the car?"

"Motorcycle." Slurring, she fought to get the words out. "Two blocks over, small blue shed."

That's all I needed. Lifting Andrea over my shoulder in a fireman's carry, I pulled Kara to her feet and banded my arm around her waist. I took off as fast as I could, essentially dragging Kara along. She had some control but very little, and it was fading fast.

At the end of the row, she murmured a weak, "right." We

were close, and as I rounded the next bend, the blue structure came into sight.

In the shed, I could at least search for the capsule under
Kara's skin. If I could see, taste, or smell the chemical, we
had a chance to survive. I couldn't take her back to Ahmed's.
Either way, I wouldn't let her die.

24

KEEGAN

THE HEAT ROSE to uncomfortable levels as the minutes ticked by in the small shed. Andrea moaned on the floor, where I'd dropped her after smacking her with my gun. After securing her hands, I searched her. There wasn't another phone, just the one used to activate the poison. I found nothing else of importance.

I withdrew my med pack from my bag while my fury boiled and mixed with the oppressive heat inside. She was the woman Kara had trusted with our child. I wanted to make her pay. Not only that, but if a similar capsule was in our daughter...

I had Kara's tight cargo pants pulled down around her knees, the pads of my fingers feeling along her thighs, searching for anything under her skin. Just enough light to see trickled in from the vents near the roof. The ground where she lay was dusty but not filthy, and I was grateful. I trailed my hand along her leg. There were a few hairline scars from old wounds. That's where I focused first. It would have been easy to reopen one and insert the delivery agent.

"Hurry," Kara whispered, her coloring having taken on

an alarming gray cast. The drug was fast acting, and I had no doubt it would seize her vocal cords soon.

Andrea's eyelids blinked open in the dim light, and I let my voice carry the full force of what I wanted to do to her. "Where is it?"

Andrea jerked as if I'd struck her.

"Stop, Keegan." Kara caught my gaze. She barely had control of her neck and voice. The rest of her body was limp and would not obey her command. "Why are you accusing Andrea?"

I'd found the application on Andrea's phone, and before that, noticed her fumbling with it before Kara fell. She had not. It was time to awaken Kara to who her nanny truly served. Brushing the damp hairs from Kara's forehead, I braced for the illusion I'd have to shatter. "Because she's the one who triggered the poison. The app was open on her phone."

"What?" Her voice shook, and she gagged as her gaze jerked to Andrea. "Why—oh, God... Did you do something to Lily?"

Andrea's face softened slightly. "No, never. And I wasn't the one who implanted it. Ahmed told me that if you attempted to escape, I should press that button. I did it for your safety."

"Ahmed? You're on a first-name basis?" She coughed, and her eyes rolled back.

"Stay with me, Ankara." She was a fighter. My fingers skimmed over a long scar under her hip bone. That's when I felt it. Not more than a half inch in length, it was beneath the middle portion of the mark, easily mistaken for scar tissue. But there wasn't any damage under the rest of the silvery line.

I could guess how close Andrea and Ahmed were by the

way her voice softened when she said his name. I would let Kara put the pieces together. The betrayal would be painful. We both had a hard time with trust, and she'd let Andrea in. What to do with her would be a problem. We couldn't leave her there, and we weren't going to bring her with us, either.

Riffling through my pack, I found the small knife and wiped it down with an alcohol pad then did the same to Kara's skin. "Small cut," I warned her, not that it would bother her. We'd had so much worse done to us that it would barely register.

Kara's breathing slowed, each inhalation more difficult than the last. Dammit—I needed answers. "What the hell is poisoning her?" I growled at Andrea as Kara slipped into unconsciousness.

"I-I don't know. Ahmed said it would stop her. He wouldn't kill her. I was to call him when she went down, and he'd handle her from there." Her dark eyes flashed with determination. "I did it to find Lily. Where is she?"

I ignored her. But I didn't relish listening to her, either. After binding her mouth so she would stay silent, I turned my focus back to Kara.

Blood welled as the knife separated Kara's skin on her hip. I clenched a penlight between my teeth and shone it on the incision, pulling her skin to spread it wider. *There.* A tiny tube was visible. With tweezers, I gently clamped on to the capsule and slowly drew it from her.

A small section gaped on one side where the vessel had released its contents. Bringing it to my nose, I ignored the coppery smell of Kara's blood and inhaled to try to isolate the elements. There had to be something that would clue me into how to save her.

Fuck. It was odorless but induced paralysis. If it was what I thought, she would be okay. I washed the incision then butterfly bandaged it before covering it with gauze and tape. Yanking the medical bag from my pack, I made a makeshift IV to flood her system with saline and flush the drug from her body, I hoped. After checking her vitals, I prepared to wait it out and get answers from Andrea.

The chances were high it wasn't a lethal chemical, but one we'd experienced in our youth with the Dark Wings. I recognized the way the paralyzing drug spread from her limbs up to her neck. She was sluggish and not without the possibility of movement, but she would have felt weighted down, and movement was very difficult to execute. The vulnerability while under the drug was horrifying, but she was safe with me. I wouldn't let anything happen to her. I'd run my hands over every inch of her body after butterflying the incision on the off chance there were other booby traps Ahmed had subjected her to without her awareness.

I readjusted her clothes then slipped one of my T-shirts under her head to act as a pillow. We had to wait it out. There was no way I could keep her safe on the motorcycle. Another hour notched by, and the heat inside the shed climbed even higher, the small vents below the roofline doing little to cool the interior.

Now and then, hurried footsteps caused Andrea to tense, to appear hopeful. I trained my gun on her. She didn't make a sound, although I didn't trust that she wouldn't, even though I'd gagged her.

25

KEEGAN

With slow movements, I unbound Andrea's mouth. I'd positioned her against the side of the shed, and her legs stretched out in front of her. Crowding her, I rested a knife at her throat and let her see my dark intent.

"Do you know who I am?"

A tremor ran through her, but she answered, "Yes."

"Then you know what I'm capable of."

Immobile, Kara watched from her position on the ground. I needed to make sure there wasn't anything else lacing the drug. I had my suspicions. My guess was that Ahmed had inserted Andrea into the household as the nanny, rather than Kara having chosen and hired her.

We couldn't stay there, but I had no idea how I would get both women out in the shape they were in. For now, it would have to do. A bruise formed on the side of Andrea's head. The gag was gone, but the zip ties remained.

I glanced between the two women. It was time to rip the Band-Aid off of Kara's perception of Andrea.

The tip of my knife swept up Andrea's cheek, scraping but not drawing blood. Her eyes widened, and terror shone there in the dim light. I kept my voice low and even. "You're going to answer truthfully."

I pressed the blade against her forehead, where her hairline began, stopping shy of piercing her. She'd had the app on her phone to activate the drug, so it was obvious she was working for Ahmed. What I needed to do was kill any sympathy or misplaced loyalty that Kara had for her.

"You don't work for Kara, do you? You're loyal to Ahmed."

Her gaze darted to Kara, and I added pressure to the blade. Blood welled then fell in a fast stream from the shallow wound. That's why I chose to cut there first. Head wounds bled a lot, and psychologically, that would frighten her. "Is that true?"

"Yes."

"Yes, what?"

"I work for Ahmed, not Kara."

There was more. I could practically smell it. "What's the other reason why you're in Ahmed's home?"

Andrea pressed her mouth tightly together, leaching the color from her lips. I placed another slice along her forehead, and she cried out. I had zero patience for her. Blood dripped into her left eye.

"I'm his mistress," she gasped. Shadows swirled in her right eye, and her features hardened. "And when Kara isn't there, I'll remain to raise Lily as my own daughter."

"My mother?" Kara's voice gained strength.

I glanced at her over my shoulder. Her finger twitched— the saline was doing its job and flushing out the chemical.

"It was always me he wanted." Andrea's dark eyes gleamed in satisfaction.

I was done listening and clipped her with the butt of my gun again. She crumpled at my feet. Kara didn't need to listen to any more of her betrayal. That was more than enough for her to leave Andrea behind.

"I have a Jeep that's not too far." I brushed a few strands of Kara's hair behind her ear. "I won't be long."

There hadn't been noise outside the shed for some time. Although there were men with machine guns crawling all over the place, I hoped that most had left that particular area. Once I retrieved the Jeep, we should be able to leave without being spotted.

After scanning the area outside the shed's door, I raced through the alley and to a location several blocks away. The Jeep was exactly where I'd left it. Our luck was holding, which continued to shock me. With a ball cap pulled low on my head, I twisted the key, and the engine sparked to life. I drove at a slow pace toward the shed, careful not to raise any suspicion. My heart steadied when the blue structure came into sight without machine-gun-toting soldiers surrounding it.

Back inside, I bent and lifted Andrea over my shoulder, not wanting to leave her behind to give away anything about our escape. The Jeep had a hollowed-out back seat, perfect for stashing the unconscious woman. They were expecting three people, I hoped. After she was secure, I helped Kara. Some mobility was returning to her limbs.

"The bike." Kara notched her head in the direction of the sweet Ducati. I wanted to ride it, but we couldn't fit Andrea onto it with us.

"We'll come back for it." And we would. There was no doubt in my mind that someone would take note of us in the Jeep. We would have to ditch it eventually. Then the bike would come in handy.

"Wait." She raised a hand. "I have weapons in the tool chest inside and more in the saddlebags."

I paused then opened the storage. Amidst several guns and knives, there were two helmets, hers and a tiny one for Lily. Seeing that gutted me. She'd planned for a fast exit. I cleared out the weapons as well as her leather jacket and a few items of clothing. Enough time had passed that she'd gained more strength and was sitting when I turned back. The makeshift IV was empty, and she pulled the needle from her arm.

I took the bag from her before securing a bandage over where the needle had pierced her skin. After packing up the medical supplies and putting on my pack, I helped her with her coat and left the helmet for the time being. The dark Plexiglas visor would have hidden her. I hoped the jacket and scarf I tied on her head would be enough to divert attention.

Wrapping my arm around her waist, we cleared the door, and I secured it behind us. Later, I would come back for that bike.

I lifted her into the Jeep and secured her seat belt. Before rounding the vehicle, I handed her a gun and extra clips. We took off through the alley at a moderately fast pace. The sound of a vehicle would alert some of the men, and they would investigate.

We didn't have long to wait before that happened. The cry went up. Shots were fired. Some guards jumped in cars and quickly were in pursuit of us. Kara swiveled to the side and returned fire. I wove along the street, making us a harder target. I took a turn hard, careening around the corner. She clung to the roll bar while shooting. We had to shake them before leading them to where I was staying.

On the main road, I opened up the engine, and we flew. Shouts faded behind us. More would pursue us when they got their cars. Hopefully, by then, we'd have enough distance between us.

I pushed the Jeep to go faster. Her hand shot out and plastered against my leg as we swerved. After another few miles, we would circle back toward town, far enough from where they should be traveling.

Adrenaline pumped through my veins as the wind tangled my hair around my head. I wished we could keep going with no need to return. There was freedom in the speed and the countryside flying by. I wanted so much more for us.

Even though we were in a high-speed chase, our lives hanging in the balance, I wouldn't have had it any other way. We were together, and that's more than I had ever hoped would happen. She fit in more ways than one. Connected by our past and bound by Lily, we finally stood a chance—if we could escape.

I estimated another few minutes before I would turn us around and go back to my team's most recent safe house. We would stash the Jeep in the empty garage. There could be no visible trail, no threat to those who sheltered us.

And before we left the country, we would have to deal with Andrea.

26

KARA

I PACED the small room where Keegan was staying. My hip stung from the incision Keegan had made. I should have been shocked that the capsule had been there, but I wasn't. The scar tissue had done a pretty good job of hiding it, and I knew when it had to have happened— during a botched job when I'd been ambushed and outnumbered.

An hour had already passed, and despite some weakness and a lingering headache, I wasn't in bad shape, but I was so very angry. Andrea's presence in the room with us ate at my soul. *How could she betray us? I trusted her with my daughter!*

The sound of a pan banging shifted my focus away from Andrea, and I was relieved. Janie and José's son had died fighting to keep the few dollars and bag of food he'd had on him. I knew the homeowners and ached for them because of the loss of their son. Our government wasn't doing anything to improve the lives of the people, and the streets weren't safe at night.

When we went inside, Janie had broken down. After

hugs, I'd filled them in and made sure they wouldn't breathe a word to anyone. Their safety was paramount to me.

The heady smell of empanadas stuffed with salty white cheese and ground beef wafted from the other room. Janie and José were moving around in the kitchen, preparing the meal. We would sit and eat with them despite Keegan's trepidation. It would be rude not to, and we could spare an hour since we hadn't planned to move around until nightfall.

Keegan had kneeled by Andrea, a syringe in his hand.

"What are you doing?"

He cleaned her arm then inserted the needle before answering me. "It's a mild sedative, enough to keep her unconscious for a few hours. It protects these people here and wherever we take her so she can't tell Ahmed much."

"Oh." I hadn't even thought to ask if he had anything like that. Immediately, I felt better about being in Janie and José's home. Then I remembered the files. "With everything that's gone on, I forgot to show you want I found." I reached into the cup of my bra and maneuvered the push-up cushion to reveal the pockets. With the tips of my fingers, I eased the thumbnail drives and drone out. "Here." I dropped them into his hand.

"What the fuck, Kara!" His head snapped up after looking into the sharpie cap. "You had this on you? Close to your skin?"

I shrugged. "How else did you expect me to get it out?" Anger climbed my spine. *That's the thanks I get for risking my neck riffling through Ahmed's office?*

"Goddammit." He set everything down with care before scrubbing his face with his hands. "You could've gotten killed. We don't know what this one is. It could have been an explosive, or poison could have leaked and gotten onto your skin." He was scared for me.

I laid my hand on his bicep. "I'm okay, and we, not Ahmed, have that now."

"I—" He gripped my shoulders and pulled me to him. "I can't lose you."

In his arms, I trembled. I wanted a future with him, but he couldn't keep me safe all the time—I was a grown woman. "It's what we do." I kept my voice soft. "We take risks. I would do it all over again to keep Ahmed from having something that dangerous."

After another tight squeeze, he let me go, and I gave him a few minutes to come to terms with what I'd said. He knew I was right. Keegan bent down, withdrew a metal box, and put the drone in it. We would be okay, so long as we made it out of Venezuela.

"Before we leave"—Keegan's gaze met and held mine—"we could call Lily. I'm sure she's worried about you."

Tears sprung to my eyes. "Yes."

He withdrew his cell and made the call. After he chatted for a brief moment with one of the men he worked with and told him about the drone, he handed me his phone. My hand shook as I accepted it. All that mattered to me was that my daughter was free and safe. "Lily?"

"Mama! Aunt Liv has clay! I made a bowl. Aunt Stel and Aunt Mari made *potions*. Are you coming now?"

I almost fell to my knees at the sound of her excited prattle. "Potions?"

"Glitter and something. Mine's pink. It's fairy dusk, Mama."

"Dust," a woman in the background said. "Fairy dust."

"I said that." Lily's response was muffled as she talked to the other person.

The exasperation in her voice made me laugh, and tears fell from my eyes in a happy stream.

"When'll you be here?"

"As soon as I can, baby girl."

"Daddy wants to talk to you," Lily said in a rush. "Love you, Mama."

"I love you more, my sweet." Samir had to have been why she wasn't hysterical in a new environment. I held in the urge to curl into a ball and cry at the sheer relief of hearing that my baby girl was happy and safe.

"Kara." Samir's gentle voice sent another wave of gratitude through me.

"Hi, Samir. She sounds good." I swiped at my cheeks, whisking the tears away.

"She is. Are you on your way?"

"Soon. We have one thing to take care of first. How's David?" David of Meyer Ancestry Labs was to Samir what Keegan was to me—he was Samir's world. They'd met last year during a conference Samir attended. After David hired Samir as a consultant, they worked closely through David's business, and a relationship quickly developed. "Have you told him?"

Samir had helped me enough, and when I insisted he not come back, I'd meant for him to find his happiness with the love of his life, David. Samir had read between the lines. We'd spoken many nights about what-ifs when we were alone together.

"No." He sighed. "David had a hacker attempt to download sensitive files yesterday, and he's at the office, working with IT to ensure their data is safe."

My gaze shot to Keegan's. "I just had a horrible thought. Do you think that's the reason why Ahmed was interested in Samir's connection to Meyer Ancestry Labs? To establish a back door into David's confidential DNA records?"

"I wouldn't put anything past your father, but what

would he gain from doing that?" The hatred Samir had for Ahmed clung to his words.

Keegan swore and motioned for the phone. "Put Chris on," he snapped before he hit the speaker button.

Seconds passed before another voice filled the air. "Chris," Keegan barked. "Would the drones respond to DNA coding?"

"They could," Chris confirmed. "If they have genetic samples for any of those in the council or even the president, they could infect one of the members with a targeted virus that would morph into a deadly virus when they sneezed around the intended victims. It would eliminate the need to go near the meeting at all and provide a path of escape and limited detection for the one who set the process in motion."

I took a breath. "That would be an ingenious method to cloak both Ahmed and the Venezuelan president's hands from being dirty with pending deaths." More and more of the puzzle pieces fell into place. "They must have gained intel about the agenda of the meeting."

"That's the consensus," Chris said. "They were voting on adding the Venezuelan president to the kill list. I'm not sure if there was anyone else, too, but that alone would topple the current government to make way for new blood." Chris's voice was muffled as he spoke to someone else. "I'll get a list of the clients who have used David Meyer's ancestry testing."

After disconnecting the call, Keegan put the capped syringe into his bag, probably to dispose of later. "Help me wipe down the room. After we eat with the family, we've got to go."

I helped him clean all the surfaces while trying to make sense of his conversation with Chris. "I don't understand why one person coughing at a meeting would cause such harm."

"We're worried that Hugo plans to program one of the nano drones to infect a specific carrier's DNA with a virus. It would be aimed to attack another with a known DNA sequence. When the germs are released into the air, there could be a secondary function of the infection that unlocks and targets the intended recipient with a deadly cocktail that would result in death."

"Ahmed relies heavily on his position and has a great deal of power and influence with his connection to the president." I cleared my throat. It all made sense. "And it's something I could see Ahmed involved in."

Janie called to us, and we paused our discussion to have a quick meal with them. I found out all Keegan and Jack had done for them in return for shelter. I think I fell in love with him even more. *Love? Oh God, I do love him.*

For as long as I could remember, I'd wanted him, looked up to him. But after he'd saved Lily and risked his life for us, I couldn't fight the hold he had on my heart any longer. Shoving my recent revelation aside, I helped Janie clean up before we said our goodbyes. Keegan and I went back into the room one last time.

Keegan waved to the lump against the wall. "We need to figure out what to do with Andrea."

I nodded, mulling it over. "We have to get her out of here before she wakes or hears anything. I wouldn't risk my friends, should she decide to tell Ahmed."

"Do you have any suggestions? I planned to dump her in an alley somewhere."

"I know two people who are mixed up in express kidnapping. We could leave her with them." It was risky, but we had to do something. "They're not dangerous, not really.

Just trying to provide for their families." Again, I glanced at Andrea's still form. "We can take her to them."

"I'm not sure this is the best time of day for us to venture out."

Keegan was right, but Andrea couldn't stay with us. "I won't risk them." I notched my head to indicate the owners.

He crossed the room to my side. "You need a disguise before we go out. See if your friend has a scarf for your hair and a pair of sunglasses. And different clothes, too. Maybe a dress?"

That would not have been something I would ordinarily wear, so it made perfect sense. "I'll be quick."

"I'll get Andrea into the Jeep. Meet me there." Keegan picked her up and hefted her over his shoulder.

It took less than five minutes for Janie to get what I needed and then for me to change. I slid into the passenger seat next to Keegan, who'd put a hat and sunglasses on. His hair curled in loose waves, and I longed to run my fingers through it. I loved his hair. It was so different than the crew cut he'd worn when I'd first met him. That and his sheer size changed how he'd looked all those years ago. He did not resemble the boy who'd protected me while I slept in a deadly training camp.

"Where are we going?" he asked.

I gave him directions to Raphi's. They would be holed up in an abandoned building. I didn't like what they did, but at least they never targeted people whose families couldn't afford to pay something. We weren't far, and it didn't take long to arrive.

Ahmed's soldiers were not in the streets, but I wouldn't let my guard down. Keegan had led them to believe we'd fled in the opposite direction. They wouldn't have expected us to loop back right under Ahmed's nose. Soldiers would be crawling over the ports and airport. Eventually, they would come back and look for us. I hoped that we'd be long gone by then.

I wished we were on the Ducati, with my arms wrapped around Keegan. I wanted to be closer, to touch him. After we got rid of Andrea, I hoped we would take the bike as our means of escape.

"Turn here." I pointed down a side street in an industrial area. A man leaned against the doorway of a mechanic's shop. The next few shops were boarded up. As we neared the building where Raphael would be, I had Keegan slow. "Pull around the side."

When he pulled to a stop beside the building, I hopped out. I rapped my knuckles on the door. "Open up, Raphi. It's Kara."

I felt rather than heard Keegan. The heat of his body loomed over me, protective and fierce. While I found that sexy as hell, I didn't need him watching my back.

Raphi opened the door. His gun jerked up and his eyes bulged when he took in Keegan. "Who is this?"

I smacked his gun down. "He's with me." My frown matched Raphi's. "We have a drop-off for you."

"Oh? What's with the disguise?" He grinned, and his posture relaxed. "You're joining the cause? Finally getting away from the big bad dad?"

I rolled my eyes. "The getup is because I'm out of Ahmed's house and away from his influence, but not by his grace. And I'm not joining your business." I pursed my lips. That wasn't entirely true. "Except for this one little favor. I need you to hold someone for me. Ahmed won't pay, but you can try to ransom her."

"What kind of trouble are you leaving at my door?"

Keegan stepped forward, and I instinctively leaned back.

God, I wanted nothing more than to leave that place and be with him. With Samir and me both soon to be free, I might be able to live the dream of being with Keegan for real. But it was not the time. "Andrea, my daughter's nanny, betrayed us to Ahmed. Please hold her for three days. You can try to get money from Ahmed if you want. If you'd rather stay under the radar, keep her blindfolded, but release her after that time."

I withdrew a wad of cash. "For your trouble."

"I would have done it for free for you, Kara." Raphi's features tightened. "Get far from here."

I flung myself at Raphi, wrapping my arms around him in a tight hug. When I pulled back, my eyes had misted. "Take care."

Keegan retreated to the Jeep as Raphi and I exchanged our goodbyes. Andrea was over his shoulders, her wrists bound and eyes covered. After he passed her to one of the men Raphi waved over, we got back in the Jeep and sped off.

"Are you okay?" Concern laced his words.

I melted even more. "I will be." If only we could escape Venezuela without any more problems.

27

KEEGAN

WIND RUSHED through the open Jeep. I glanced at Kara. Her features, or what I could see of them in the dim light of evening, were tense. We'd had a pretty good run of luck. We were so close to going back to Maine, but I had a bad feeling it was about to end.

We didn't need anything to leave aside from our escape boat. I had supplies in my backpack. She had the clothes on her back. When we arrived in Maine, Liv and the others would make sure Kara had whatever she needed. I maneuvered the vehicle through the streets. We'd put a good ten miles between us and Andrea. Kara remained silent by my side. I knew she was scanning the area, too, looking for an ambush.

"Not much longer, and we'll be at the water." I wanted to reassure her. Aside from a possible run-in with patrols, there was a small chance we would have to wait for our boat to arrive. Either way, we were one step closer to getting out of Venezuela. I never wanted to come back.

"I hope so." Her hand tightened on the gun tucked against her thigh.

"When we get—"

My words were lost in the metal on metal explosion as another car T-boned us on Kara's side. The Jeep lurched then spun. The seat belt bit into my chest as the accident registered. We skidded then were hit again. The Jeep rolled. Kara's scream filled my ears over the impact. My head rang when the Jeep stopped, and my left side felt as if it had been sandpapered off by concrete.

Reality seeped in, more slowly than I would have liked. Kara hung from her belt, unconscious and listing toward me. With my good hand, I released the button for the seat belt and fell partially onto the road, my legs still inside. I grasped for my gun.

Hands curled around me, and I was pulled from the Jeep, the weapon stripped from my grip. Ignoring the pain, I lurched to my feet, and their hands fell away. There were three men. Two had guns pointed at me, and at the center stood Jamal.

I recognized one of the Dark Wing soldiers. A menacing gleam shone in his dead eyes. There was history between the soldier, Kara, and me. All those years before, in the camp, I'd ensured her safety from him at night. There were others that had caused concern, but he was the worst of the lot.

The soldier approached the overturned vehicle, and I reacted. No way would I let him touch Kara. As I lunged, my fingers curled around a knife in a side pocket. I let it fly. With a thunk, it found its target. Blood welled then spurted around the protrusion in his neck. A wet gurgle sounded as he staggered back. I should have done that a long time ago.

Too focused on Kara, he hadn't anticipated my action. Mistake. That left two. Easier to manage. I lunged to the fallen soldier and relieved him of the scimitar strapped to his side.

"You shouldn't have done that." Jamal motioned to the other man to retrieve Kara then attacked.

I ducked as Jamal swung a curved sword at my head. We engaged, blade against blade, and Jamal had the upper hand. The clang of metal rang through the streets. Our fight was practiced due to many years of training together. But I'd learned new things and was younger and quicker. Then again, I hadn't landed a single blow.

Throughout our deadly dance, I wanted to check on Kara but couldn't spare the focus. Jamal was a skilled warrior, and it seemed he was besting me. I had to step up my game. I was better than that.

Pain lanced my arm as his blade grazed off it. *Dammit.* I bent and weaved. We traded blows in a combination of martial arts and street fighting. It could have gone on for a long time and needed to end. With each movement, I assessed him for weakness. Jamal had few, but as a teenager, I'd managed to best him once. I would do it again.

Metal sang as I flipped his sword into the air. In an arc, I sliced my knife down and reopened the scar on his cheek. A river of red flowed down his face, but he didn't react. He jerked another blade free of his clothing and whipped it at me. Pivoting, I almost avoided it. The weapon lodged in my arm. Blood dripped from the wound then off my fingers. We circled one another, ready to attack again.

Neither of us would tire anytime soon, not until one of us lay at the other's feet. With a twist, I landed a kick to his chest as he jerked the blade from my arm. Two steps back, and we regrouped.

"Stop or she dies."

I froze. Not taking my gaze off Jamal, I caught a glimpse

of Kara, still unconscious and on her knees. A stream of dark red trailed from her temple. A large lump had formed on her forehead.

The other soldier had a fistful of hair, holding her head up. Her eyes remained closed. But the knife at her throat wasn't something I could ignore. There was a chance they wouldn't kill her, that Ahmed wanted her alive. But I wasn't sure. That was enough to still my hand. *Goddammit!*

We were in a world of trouble.

28

KEEGAN

BUILDINGS THEN HOUSES flew by as the SUV bumped along uneven roads. I sat in the back with Jamal, who pointed a gun at me the entire way. Sweat beaded on my forehead as my gaze strayed to Kara time and again. *Please be okay.* She hadn't regained consciousness yet, and her body listed to the side in the front seat, making the driver's job an easy one. If we'd had a few minutes, I could've made sure she wasn't seriously injured.

Zip ties cut into my wrists. Thankfully, they'd secured our wrists so that our hands were bound in front. Foolish, especially from them. Jamal must have grown complacent over the years, running things by focusing on cushy cash-rich jobs like the ones with Ahmed and not actively partici-pating. They would never have made mistakes like that when I was there. It was possible that they were looking for more sport, should we attempt to escape. Then anything concerning our delivery, whether dead or severely wounded, would be game.

We were headed to Ahmed's, and ultimately to my execution.

I'd faced worse odds. We would get out of this.

Our chances would be better if we didn't cross over Ahmed's property line. Every few seconds, my gaze strayed back to Kara. I thought I'd seen a twitch from her but wasn't sure. In case she was coming to, I had to keep Jamal's focus on me.

"Ahmed hired you. For what?" Jamal's dead eyes bore into mine, the antagonizing question not making a bit of difference. I had to keep trying. "To be an errand boy?"

"Kara will go back to her father. She is his problem. You, on the other hand..." A malicious smirk curled his lips. "Hugo had his chance. I'll own you again."

Interesting that Kara didn't belong to the Dark Wings. "Ah, so my fate is in your hands. Is that it?" It was never going to happen. I created my own destiny and had since the day I escaped Jamal's camp.

He inclined his head, answering my question.

"Hugo's close by?" Chris had said he cleared customs. I wanted to make sure he hadn't returned to Venezuela.

"He'll be back."

"My debt to you is paid." My uncle had worked a deal with Jamal when I was a kid, locking me into a contract of sorts with the Dark Wings—basically, they owned me until I turned sixteen. Then, my uncle wanted those rights over my life to revert back to him. But I'd escaped days before my sixteenth birthday. Hugo owed Jamal for those stolen days, not me. "The agreement is no longer between us, but between you and Hugo." I needed to ensure his thought process wouldn't extend to us when we escaped.

"True." He smirked. "But fortunate nonetheless. There are assassinations you'll fulfill when the time is right. As for Hugo, I'll deal with him when the time comes. His life has always been mine." He slapped the side of my cheek in a rough pat. "Nothing for you to worry over."

"And the drones?"

"Why do you care?"

"Passes the time." Conversation wasn't Jamal's favorite pastime. Torture was.

Jamal shrugged. "Those are Hugo's responsibility. Delivering his daughter ends my obligation with Ahmed." His gaze shifted to Kara for a brief moment. "Pity. I could have used both of you as my soldiers."

"We're not mindless servants." I made a point of visually tracing the reopened scar on his face—the original wound from my handiwork years ago. "I doubt things would work in your favor."

"Perhaps, but everyone has a breaking point." He pursed his lips. "We would find yours... again."

I bared my teeth and jerked toward him, stopped short by the seat belt. Neither he nor the driver wore theirs. Jamal laughed, and the driver glanced at me in the rearview mirror.

Kara came to life and grabbed the driver's gun. With force, she slammed it against his head. A dull thud sounded as she struck him. He slumped, and then we swerved.

Kara pushed on the unconscious man's leg. We careened forward. The soldier's body leaned against the wheel, keeping us marginally on the same path, at least for the time being.

Jamal's focus was on me. He lifted his gun and aimed. I had to do something, quickly.

I ducked to the side as much as I could as he pulled the trigger. The heat from the bullet burned along the side of my head. For half a second, I fumbled with the seat belt. It released. There was only a matter of seconds before he shot me. I could see Kara's hands swinging toward the back. *No!* I didn't want Jamal to shift his attention to her. Jerking my hands up, I knocked into the hand that held his gun.

The next shot went wide. Kara fired as Jamal did so again. Her shot hit home, but off-center. Blood pooled near Jamal's collarbone. It hadn't been a kill shot.

Jamal took aim at her head. With a roar, I launched myself at him. We tumbled from the vehicle just as Kara kicked the driver out then took his place.

The SUV sped a short distance forward before Kara slammed her foot on the brake, and the vehicle came to a screeching halt. I landed on top of Jamal. Delivering a swift right hook to the underside of his chin, I pushed off him. Blood sprayed from his flayed wound, and his eyes rolled back.

Jumping to my feet, I flung myself into the SUV. Kara wasted no time. She reversed the car, and we ran over Jamal's body. I arched my eyebrows and held her gaze.

"What?" A sheepish smile curved her lips. "Now he doesn't have any hold on you."

Laughter roared through my chest as I threw my head back as she hit the gas, jolting forward and running over my enemy once more.

"Where to?" Her voice was lighter with Jamal as road kill behind us.

"We're about five miles out. Head toward the ocean, then I'll direct you." We would be on our way home soon. My only concern was that our transportation wouldn't arrive for a while.

After fifteen minutes, we pulled up to the small alcove amidst trees and bushes. As I suspected, the boat hadn't arrived, but I was confident it would. Lifting my backpack from the vehicle, I withdrew my cell and connected to home. Liam answered on the second ring.

"We're at the exit. Any news?" He knew what I meant.

"Couple hours out. Hang tight."

We made ourselves comfortable to wait it out. Neither Jack nor Hawk had had a single problem leaving. We would be okay.

Kara spat blood on the sandy dirt, and my gut dropped. Stepping close, my hands skimmed along her ribs to her stomach, gently prodding. She slapped my hands away. "I'm fine. It's a cut in my mouth."

"Let me look." I set down my pack with the intent of getting the med kit out to clean the gash on her forehead.

Kara sighed but complied, sitting on the ground and leaning against a tree. "Okay, Doc."

I knew she wanted to roll her eyes, but her head injury must have prevented the motion. Doing that while nauseous and dizzy could have been the thing that pushed her over the edge to puking. With care, I cleaned then bandaged the wound on her head. It would be a while until we could get ice on the bump to reduce the swelling. Instead, I gave her some pain meds.

She popped them into her mouth and swallowed them with the water I handed to her. "When is this boat supposed to arrive? Or are we bait?"

"No, we'll be safe. They're probably waiting for it to get darker. Best guess, I'd say they'll be here around two in the morning." Jamal's comment nagged at me. "You were never initiated into the Dark Wings?" I had to make sure for her sake and for Lily's, should one of the other men rise up and take over.

"No." She scooted closer and leaned against me. "Ahmed

insisted they train me only. He hired Jamal for the messier jobs he didn't want any ties to."

"Murder."

"Basically. I worked alongside the Dark Wings a few times, but I'm not officially a member."

"And Hugo? What is his connection to your father? Has he been at the house often?"

I worried about Lily's exposure to him.

"I met him once, briefly. That was fairly recent. Ahmed kept his business as secreted away as possible. I was only to execute his orders, not be included in the reasons why. The last one was simple: recover the pack Hugo had and him, if it was convenient." She shrugged against me. "I don't know if they go way back or if the connection was through Jamal."

"What does your father stand to lose, should the National Security Council have the Venezuelan president assassinated? Does he want to insert himself in that position?"

"As president? No. He has the best of both worlds, just enough freedom to do whatever he chooses, in business and personally, with the position he holds now. As a favored advisor, he will do what he's required by the president or on his own to ensure things remain as they are."

"Chris uncovered a deposit made from one of the Venezuelan president's accounts into Ahmed's."

"Makes sense." Kara sighed then tangled our fingers together. We both needed the contact, the connection. "Ahmed will hire the muscle, and the dirty work will not touch the president."

My blood sizzled. We were running out of time.

29

KEEGAN

THE BOAT HAD FINALLY ARRIVED, and Kara and I fled Caracas to Aruba. From there, we boarded a jet flown by the pilot who filled in when Trev couldn't transport us. We had a few hours before we touched down on the airstrip in Maine. Kara stood and stretched. She'd changed into jeans and a long-sleeved black T-shirt that rode up and revealed a sliver of enticing skin above her jeans. I ran my thumb over her exposed skin before tugging her to me by her hip.

A slow, sexy smile curved her lips as she lowered herself onto my lap. We were both sore from the car crash and the ensuing fights, but that didn't stop either of us from getting as close as we could. All my injuries faded at the feel of her as her arms wound around my neck and she leaned against me. Her fingers toyed with the hair at the base of my neck.

We didn't need words. I wrapped my arms around her waist and held her tight, neither of us needing words, too exhausted from everything that we'd been through. She relaxed into me even more and a sense of peace came over me as her breathing deepened and I realized she'd fallen asleep. There was so much she and I had been through, and even with the bad, we trusted each other enough to be vulnerable.

I dozed on and off until we landed. She never woke. Transporting her to the car went smoothly, I didn't want to let her go. Not now, not ever.

Kara slept as I drove along the roads, pressed against my side, and I let out a breath of relief that she was safe and with me in the States—away from her father. I turned onto the driveway that lead to Savage Wind Farm, where Liam and Liv lived. It was also the Gray Ghost Security home base.

We'd left Caracas under cover of night and arrived in Maine close to dinnertime. My stomach growled at the thought of a home-cooked meal. Then there was Lily. On the flight, Kara and I had strategized about how we would tell her about me being her dad. We wouldn't do it right away. There were too many changes going on, and neither one of us wanted to cause her any further stress.

Kara seemed to be under the impression that she would have to find somewhere else to live when the whole thing was over, but that wasn't happening. They would stay with me. It could take a while to convince her, but I knew she would come around and see my point. It was time to establish roots in Maine, where the majority of our team was. It would be the best place to protect Kara and Lily from Ahmed, should he entertain ideas of retrieving them.

After shutting the engine down, I gently nudged Kara then gave into my need to touch her and tucked a few strands of dark hair behind her ear. "We're here."

She jerked awake. "Wha—" She suddenly seemed to realize she wasn't in danger, and her body relaxed. Her gaze roamed over the sprawling farm and large home. She turned to me, and a huge smile pulled at her lips. "Lily's here?"

I nodded.

That was all she needed. She scrambled from the car and raced to the door that someone flung open. Mari stood at the threshold, her long black hair draped over one shoulder. I got out of the car, and as I rounded the back bumper, I saw that Kara had stopped short.

I climbed the three steps then stood behind her. My hand curled around her hip, tethering her to me. "Kara, this is Mari, Chris's wife."

"Mama!" A high-pitched shriek echoed from somewhere in the house, and Kara shuddered. I released her as Mari stepped to the side. Kara didn't need any prodding. She rushed inside as Lily rounded the corner from the direction of the kitchen with a smudge of what looked like flour on her cheek.

"My baby girl." Kara dropped to her knees as Lily launched herself into her mom's arms, sobbing.

They needed a few minutes, as I was sure Lily had been just as scared for her mom as Kara had been for her daughter. At only four years old, the separation and being in a new place had to have been a huge shock.

Their dark hair mingled, the shades an identical match. I squeezed Mari's shoulder as I stepped in, noting the softening of her eyes as she watched the reunion of mother and daughter. "Good to see you."

Mari gave me a quick hug. "You too. You have a few hours, then the guys are heading out."

"We have a lead?"

"We do," Mari answered before touching Kara's shoulder. "Lily and I are making cookies. Do you want to help?"

Kara agreed then stood and gave me a quick kiss on the

cheek before she turned back to her daughter. With Lily's hand in hers, she followed Mari. As they walked away, Lily turned and gave Mari and me a tiny wave, despite her sniffles and the crocodile tears still rolling down her face.

"Save me some cookies, Princess."

She giggled then skipped beside her mom as they rounded the corner. With Kara next to her, she recovered quickly, and I knew the reason. She was accustomed to her mom having to leave for dangerous missions, even if she didn't know why. Her time in Ahmed's house hadn't been what a typical little girl encountered. When Lily was out of hearing distance, I dropped my easygoing façade. "What are we dealing with?"

Jack appeared at the end of the hallway and motioned for us to join him in the back of the house. Mari shut the door behind us, and we met him in the family room. I wanted the whole thing to be finished. Despite the exhaustion clinging to my bones, I would rather get back out there if it meant swift closure. Ever since Chris had told us Hugo wasn't in Caracas any longer, the need to put him behind bars—or better yet, in a box six feet underground—felt urgent.

"Where is everyone?" I asked Jack.

The door to the patio opened, and in walked Hawk and Stella. Chris came through from the direction of the kitchen. If I looked close enough, I could see Liv's outline through a window in the oversized shed that Liam had turned into an art studio for her to sculpt in. That left several still unaccounted for. I'd hoped we would have a fairly full team.

"We're short by a few. Matt, Connor, Trev, Hayden, and Mike aren't here and won't be able to get to DC in time to help," Jack explained. "It'll just be us."

We'd had worse odds. I told myself everything would be fine. I dropped to the couch, tired from all the travel, and my arm ached where Jamal had stabbed me. Kara had patched me up while we waited for the boat, but I needed to change the dressing and get another antibiotic shot. God knew what had been living on Jamal's knife.

I dug through my bag then handed over the box with the drone and the thumbnail drives Kara had stolen. "We only need to recover five drones now."

Jack whistled as he opened the box and got a peek at the realistic-looking mosquito. "I'll let Rich know. His military connections will help him get it into the right hands."

I nodded, glad to get it out of mine. "Where's Hannah?" Jack's wife, the former Russian spy, would be a welcome addition, and I hoped she would be a part of our team for this mission. Hugo was a slippery fucker, and she could help us take him out quickly—and, of course, help to stop the robot insect attack and the subsequent unnecessary deaths.

"She's working with her Russian recruits and won't be able to help." Jack waved to my arm.

I'd changed shirts, but blood had seeped through the bandage and stained the new shirt too. "Knife wound. What recruits?"

"Russian defectors. She's expanding the program Rich started with her, and now the girl Hannah stashed in the Cook Islands is a part of the team to help discover other sleeper agents in the States."

I grunted at his response. I would deal with that information another day. Yanking on my sleeve, I tore the shirt from shoulder to elbow. "I need a med kit."

Chris got up and went in search of one. When he came back, Stella sat next to me and got to work on fixing me up. Hawk shifted so he was closer to his wife's shoulder. She winked at me, and I smirked at our sniper, who was observing everything she did. I didn't blame him. She was pretty great. Even so, I couldn't resist getting a rise out of Hawk. "You going on this one with us, too, Stel?"

Hawk's intense blue eyes bored into mine. "Came back with a death wish?"

Stel shook her head. "Knock it off, both of you. Of course, I'm not going. I'd rather spend time with that cute little girl who looks awfully like you, Keegan."

"Only her eyes, and we're not saying anything yet." I wasn't ready to have that conversation. I wanted to have a serious one with Samir, though. I wasn't exactly sure how I felt. Even though I recognized that my slow-simmering anger stemmed from envying that he'd had all those years with my girls, I'd been too stubborn to tell Kara five years before, when I'd had the chance. It was all because I'd wanted to distance myself completely from my old life, even though my heart had only ever belonged to Kara. I'd been too stupid to recognize it at the time.

"We need to get back on track," Jack said.

"Right," Chris said, opening the laptop on the coffee table.

We gathered around.

"David Meyer, the owner of the ancestry-slash-DNA company, confirmed that he does have genetic data from almost all the members of the National Security Council."

Two more members taken out would stall the vote indefinitely. Even when new members were appointed, there was a good chance the deaths wouldn't point back to Ahmed or the Venezuelan president, and the new members wouldn't vote against them.

"Do we know for a fact the database information was stolen?" Jack asked Chris.

Chris shook his head. "Not a hundred percent, no. But there is a good chance the hacker got what he was looking for. The backdoor entrance he established for the handful of minutes he was in before they locked down their security could have been enough."

"The meeting is set for tomorrow morning at nine. We need to go in assuming the secretary of the army and the secretary of energy have been infected with a virus that'll change into a secondary airborne contagion that's deadly to the others."

"All they'd need to do is sneeze?" I asked.

"Yes," Chris replied.

Stella finished up with my arm, and I thanked her.

"We were unable to locate the secretary of energy. The secretary of the army was picked up a few hours ago and is undergoing treatment for the virus he was infected with," Jack clarified.

If we didn't find the secretary of energy before he met with and unintentionally infected any of the remaining National Security Council, we would be in a world of trouble.

———

Kara

I smoothed Lily's hair as she helped Mari scoop batter into balls and place them on the cookie sheet. My hand shook at the shock of what both of us together in Maine meant: freedom for all of us, Samir, Lily, and myself. We could start over.

The enormity hit me, and I sucked in a deep breath and worked hard to control my ping-ponging emotions.

"There are my girls."

"Hi, Daddy!" Lily shouted. "We're making cookies. Want some?"

"Of course I do, sugar plum." Samir smiled then tweaked Lily's flour-coated nose.

Samir's voice broke the dam, and tears rolled down my cheeks. Before I knew it, I was in his arms, sobbing.

"Mama!" Lily tugged at my elbow, and I reached out to include her in our embrace.

"She's okay, baby," Samir reassured Lily. "She just missed us."

"I'm going to give you a few minutes and check in with the guys," Mari said before she left the kitchen.

I pulled back and flashed a watery smile at my best friend. "Can you believe it?"

Samir shook his head and laughed. "No. I didn't think we would ever be free of your father."

Lily wiggled free and went back to the cookie dough, sneaking peeks beneath her lashes at us as she went back to alternating between putting some in her mouth and then on the tray. She would probably get a tummy ache, but it would be fine.

I dropped my forehead against Samir's chest and worked hard to gain control of myself. "How's David?"

Samir's smile shone from his eyes. "Aside from work stress, he's relieved about finally making our relationship official. He's already talking about redecorating the house so it's ours and not only his choices." A shadow flitted across his features, and he cast a glance at Lily.

"It'll be okay. Please don't worry."

"I can't not be a part of her life." His voice shook.

"You always will be. There isn't any other option. We'll figure things out." I squeezed his arm. "Promise."

"What about you?" He notched his head in the direction where Keegan was, and I shrugged.

"We've been too busy running for our lives to talk much, but I'm here. Things are good." I didn't know where things would go with Keegan. I knew where I hoped they'd go, but if there was one thing I'd learned, it was that nothing could be certain. For the time being, the moments with my family were a gift, and I wanted to enjoy every second with them.

30

KEEGAN

WE ARRIVED EARLY in the morning and, with special permission from Rich, got into position around the White House grounds. Security was tight, as expected. The meeting was scheduled for a secret room accessed through the interior of the building or hidden tunnels that exited further out. We guarded the tunnel door.

I fought the urge to seek Kara out. Several feet away, she waited by another entrance in case the secretary of energy decided to go in the main. He'd been MIA by phone and wasn't at his office or residence. It was a concern. But one of the other members said it wouldn't be an issue regarding the meeting. If he was alive, he would make it.

Their agenda was a weighty one, and Rich's attempt to cancel or move the meeting had fallen on deaf ears. Their schedules were full, and a decision had to be made. The most they would agree to was having us surround the entry points and allowing us to search for the threat as we saw fit. Come hell or high water, the council and the head of the anti-terrorist department would convene.

We'd taken every precaution possible. Hugo must have

had someone on the inside or one of the recon nanoweapons monitoring their conversations, at the very least. We'd done a sweep of their offices and homes but had come up with nothing. They'd drawn a line when we attempted to track their administrative assistants. Overconfidence should not have been a luxury—apparently, they'd learned nothing from the death of their fellow council member.

The FBI was involved and crawling all over the White House and providing surveillance for the members of the National Security Council. Their presence gave the council members a level of security, of comfort, lulling them into believing that they would be safe. That wasn't quite the case, not if Hugo already got to them.

Rich had informed us that we could not, as we'd planned, disturb the wavelength on a mass scale with a frequency jammer. Apparently dignitaries were scheduled to arrive via the helicopter pad on the roof for an unrelated meeting inside the White House. That limited our use of Chris's technology. But there were key places where we'd installed the blocks.

The secretary of defense's death was proven not to be a heart attack but cardiac arrest caused by lethal poison. So intent on deciding the fate of the Venezuelan president this morning, the remaining members had forgone the extra steps we'd attempted to put in place to ensure their safety.

Jack and Hawk covered the most likely entrances, and Chris monitored for any incoming drones. If the secretary of energy didn't make it in, then our analysis suggested that Hugo would have to utilize a backup plan that would involve direct contact with nanoweapons. That would have been a riskier method as opposed to contamination via the other council member.

The meeting would determine whether the Venezuelan president would be added to the secret kill list. That wasn't our mission, nor was the outcome of their decision. Our job was to stop an attack, keep the council members safe, then capture Hugo and recover the drones.

"Got him," Hawk reported through our communication link from the parking lot. I sensed rather than heard a collective sigh of relief. Finding and holding the secretary of energy was a step in the right direction, but it wasn't over. The Center for Disease Control was on standby, and Hawk redirected the secretary to them. We'd sabotaged phase one of Hugo's plan.

It wouldn't stop a disaster from befalling us. Hugo had decimated my youth until I'd escaped, and I didn't have any doubts that he had other tricks up his sleeve.

Chris had rigged the entrances we were monitoring with anti-wavelength devices to neutralize the signals to the drones. Hugo wouldn't get any of the robot insects inside, and with the rest of the council members behind the walls, we were clear to search for him elsewhere.

I scanned the area, holding my position beside the shrub-covered tunnel entrance. Nothing moved, and my mind continued to race with what could happen. *What if Hugo landed one of the small insects on any number of employees, essentially hitchhiking on someone walking into the White House?* Then our countermeasures wouldn't matter. There were too many options for failure. I had to find Hugo.

I shifted my weight in an attempt to ease the tension. I wanted to stop him, to make him pay for more than his involvement with the drones.

"I've got a hit. Several feet away," Chris notified us.

"I'm on it." That could only have meant one thing. He'd caught Hugo on the software he used for facial recognition.

Another precaution we—Chris—had taken was using a radio transmitter capable of seizing control, basically hacking it and taking over operations for drones in flight. Not only that, but the device enabled us to detect the fingerprint of the owner of the drones infringing on the airspace.

From the shadows, I left my post, and we moved like ghosts infiltrating the grounds. I headed in the direction Chris directed. It'd been years, and I'd never known Hugo well. However, I did know what the Dark Wings would do, and he was one. That gave me some predictability in my approach and how I would flush him from his hiding place.

I spotted a small building that would provide good cover and suspected that was where he hid. The ground shook. I bent my knees to stay steady. I was two feet from the target when an explosion shattered the relatively quiet morning. Screams blended with the blast. *Dammit.* I pivoted, and my shoulder slammed into the small building. I couldn't let him escape. A quick sweep revealed no one inside. I gave the door a hard yank and was on the path in a dead run toward the tunnels.

"Far exit!" Jack shouted into our mics. "Chris and I are close."

"On an east balcony," Hawk responded.

As a sharpshooter, Hawk would be able to keep an eye on anyone entering or leaving who shouldn't. Security swarmed the area, making it difficult for us to do our job.

I cursed our misstep. We'd thought they would target the remaining members silently, with the fewest possible repercussions and ties to where they'd originated, as the first attack had. We hadn't considered the possibility that one of the robot insects was a bomb.

Hugo lacked patience and finesse, though. It was on me. I'd been away too long. I should have anticipated it. A flash of black hair in my peripheral vision alerted me to who was closing in. Kara was half a step behind me when I crashed through the gaping hole in the side of the building.

A sense of compulsion hit me, and I glanced over my shoulder. She was okay and on my heels. Determination pulled her features taut, and my mind warred with needing to keep her safe and completing the mission. She could hold her own—I knew that. But I wanted to shield her and always had.

Jack and Chris would secure the council members. Kara and I would go after Hugo. Dust filled the air. Smoke, fire, and rubble elicited fear and desperation, and people screamed and evacuated the compromised area. We wove through groups of frightened employees. Military police rushed the area. The explosion site, with its mass confusion, was perfect for what I knew Hugo had planned.

"Got them," Jack said, letting us know that he and Chris had managed to collect the council members. "Reconvene at the exit point."

We glimpsed Jack's back as he led several men toward the east exit. *Where the hell is Chris?* Agitation climbed my spine at Jack's command to abandon the chase. The primary goal, for the time being, was to get the men to safety. I glanced at Kara and noted the frustration pulling at her mouth as she turned with me. We exited the building and headed to the truck.

Panicked people raced from the exits. Sirens increased in volume as help grew closer.

Kara and I caught up, surrounding the men as much as we could. Hawk joined, taking the vulnerable side as we hurried through the corridors. Through the mob, I caught a glimpse of Chris.

Keeping the crowd from separating our group, we used

our guns to wave the majority away, shouting for them to move. The path we were on cleared enough for us to maneuver. We were close, maybe ten feet away.

Chris shoved through a group of fleeing people. The threat was still a viable one. Though he'd installed devices to interrupt wavelengths, which would render any drone flightless, it would have helped if the nanoweapons were the injectable, mosquitolike ones. It would do nothing to keep a tiny nuke or bomb from exploding nearby. If they hit the no-fly zone, there was a high probability of detonation.

The doors were wide open. Hugo could be anywhere. I scanned the area as we ran across the lawn, as did my teammates. No matter where I looked, I didn't spot him. The armored car was nearby—it wasn't what we'd arrived in; it was our best bet for getting the men out safely.

I held open the back door, and Kara followed the men in, along with Chris and then myself. Hawk climbed into the driver's seat, and Jack rode beside him. We had to get them out of there.

The truck shuddered as another loud explosion echoed from nearby. Cars careened from the bomb that'd detonated several feet to our left. He'd found us. Hawk got the vehicle back under control and increased our speed. Chris slammed several devices against the sides of the interior walls. They would interrupt the signals if the insect robots got within a certain distance. It would be enough to stop one of the robots from landing on the truck but wouldn't totally prevent damage being done. Either way, we stood a chance.

"Do something!" one of the men yelled through the divider between the back and cab.

Tires squealed. Our bodies slammed to the side. Kara pushed the men closest to her down. I did the same. Hawk got the truck straightened out and gunned the engine, and we shot forward.

Our speed climbed, and we hit a bump in the road hard enough to catch air then swerved left.

"Stay down!" I yelled. I couldn't do much for them, but if they remained on the ground, their injuries would hopefully be minimal. Legs tangled, and the four men remained on the ground. As they separated, they pressed against the sides, and I hoped they would gain stability. The only light in the armored truck's back cab came from a narrow slip that allowed the glow from the windshield in.

A loud explosion cracked to the rear passenger side, and the force pushed our heavy vehicle around and caused us to fishtail. I slammed my head into one of the down seats and cursed Hugo. The tires screeched as the vehicle listed from side to side, nearly rolling. Hawk fought and won control once more. "Stay down and hold onto something!" he shouted.

"Almost there," Jack said through our communication lines. All three of us had our guns out and ready.

Hawk jerked the heavy vehicle to the right. We bounced as the front of the truck scraped against the concrete, our speed too fast to handle the initial incline. We must have been in a parking garage. We spun at a dizzying pace.

No other attacks sounded, but I doubted we were in the clear. We had a backup plan. After a few more seconds, we would move again, just not in that truck.

Hawk slammed the vehicle into Park, and we could hear Jack and Hawk's doors opening then slamming shut. Kara pressed close, and awareness sizzled between us. Despite the danger, I was glad she was there.

The bar that held the truck's rear doors released, and the back opened. The three of us stood with our guns pointed.

The sight of Jack and Hawk had us lowering them and helping the council members from the car.

The black SUV parked next to us beeped as Chris hit the unlock button on the key fob he'd pulled from his pocket. We needed to mix things up, so Chris would drive and the rest of us piled in the back. A divider was in place between the front and the rear seats. After we squeezed in, Chris started the engine and reversed the SUV, and we began the trek down the parking garage. If Hugo or anyone working with him spotted us, they should only have registered Chris as the driver and the rest of the interior as empty. The divider had a picture of the inside without passengers on it, and a glance shouldn't have caused suspicion. The only problems would come if Chris was recognized. He pulled his Mets cap down low on his forehead.

The head of the anti-terrorist department turned to me. "What happened to the secretary of energy? Is he all right?" he whispered.

I met his concerned brown eyes and furrowed brows and offered a nod. "He's being treated as we speak."

That's all I could offer. The men turned to one another. The three of us kept watch outside, paying little attention to them. Their voices were quiet, but we heard enough, regardless.

"If there was any doubt before, this solidifies our suspicions," the head of anti-terrorism said.

"Agree," two of the council members murmured.

"We'll reconvene with a plan of action after determining the best place to strategize and secure the secretary of energy and the secretary of the army's votes."

"I'm going in first." Chris threw the SUV into Park. We'd arrived at a low-budget hotel. It was one used by the Secret Service on occasion. Chris would go in and ensure the cameras were off so there would be no record of us entering the building. Should Hugo or one of his men attempt to find us, they would see only one man exiting the car and entering the premises. He'd set the camera on a looped feed until our backup, the FBI, arrived.

There was no question in my mind that Hugo was hot on our trail.

KEEGAN

Half an hour later, Secret Service and FBI teams were inside the hotel room. Our job with the council members was done, but the mission was far from over. We'd moved quickly, but I knew Hugo wouldn't be far behind. He had a job to complete.

"Did you find him?" I couldn't stand it. The stakes were too high. *He will be caught today.*

Chris met my gaze as we filed into the parking lot of the hotel, and a smirk curved his lips. He flashed his phone's screen and showed me his tracking app. "Did you seriously doubt me?"

"Where?" Kara moved to stand alongside me.

Part of me hadn't wanted her to come—I couldn't lose her, not again. She'd finally gained her freedom. I'd had years of it. But she was stubborn, determined, and fierce, and I loved that about her. I couldn't deny her the chance to join our mission.

"He's in the parking garage where we left the armored vehicle," Chris answered.

With no other car, we piled into the SUV, decommissioning the divider that kept the passengers in the back shielded from visibility. Hawk took the wheel so Chris could freely monitor any camera he chose to hack into and use for eyes on the streets.

"He'll find the abandoned vehicle based on the dark zone if he searches for us with nanobots." Chris's devices interrupted electromagnetic fields and would disable the drones' radiofrequencies, resulting in a dark zone. "My guess is he's searching inside for us."

"Great." My blood heated. We had him. I knew it. Kara reached over and squeezed my arm in a brief show of solidarity. She knew what it meant to me to catch him. The guys did, too, but Kara had lived the life in the camp when we were young and had experienced the horrors firsthand.

"He's on the third level. Parked," Chris reported.

"It's a trap," Jack warned.

"I'm going in." I had to risk it. After all those years of hiding from Hugo, who had hijacked my innocence and my youth and had sold me to the devil, it would end there. That day. It would be a fight to the death, his or mine. One of us wouldn't leave alive. "Block off the stairwells."

"I'll go too," Kara said.

"No." I rested my palm on the side of her face, my thumb rubbing back and forth across her soft skin. I bent and kissed her slowly, savoring a single moment with her. "If something happens, Lily will need you."

"I've had worse missions." Sparks shot from her gaze and appeared to be passion mixed with defiance. "It's my decision."

Goddammit. "I know it is, but I'm asking you to stay back. Hugo is my uncle. I need to end this. If you're there and anything happens to me... I just can't, Kara. He knows there's something between us, and he'll exploit that."

A second ticked by. Then another. Finally, she nodded. "Be safe." Her hand covered mine and squeezed it.

I wanted more. I drew her close and brushed my lips over hers. Desire exploded in my veins and I deepened the kiss, promising her with my touch that I would return. In the back of my mind, the ticking clock echoed, and I broke our kiss. Our gazes held, and I cupped the side of her face one last time before we parted. The guys had moved out of the car and set up by the ramp leading down, the stairwell, and the elevator. There was no way out.

"I'll be on your six," Jack said, his tone suggesting it was nonnegotiable.

I didn't argue. If I had, they all would have gone with me, and that defeated how I wanted the whole thing to end. The anger inside from what my uncle had done was a deadly bomb waiting to explode. It was clear that Jack planned to stop me from killing Hugo and would ensure I was safe. Kara would understand, and I didn't think she would stop me.

I wasn't sure how I felt about the apparent restraint Jack's presence meant, but there wasn't time to analyze it. He was our unofficial leader, and he was looking out for me. All the guys were. That's just what we did.

With one last look, Kara got into position near the exit ramp.

My team would stop Hugo or anyone working with him from leaving. No matter what, it was the end for him. I regained control of my spiraling anticipation and made my way up the dim, gray ramp with absolute focus.

The parking garage was silent. I crept forward, scanning the parked cars and around the dingy concrete floors for signs of him. We'd left the armored car two stories below. It had only taken a small amount of time to drop the council members off in the safe house location with the FBI, so we'd arrived shortly after him.

I sensed him first—a blur of motion to my left. My instincts took over, and I ducked. His swing narrowly missed my head. In a sweep, he knocked my gun to the floor with a clatter.

I struck hard and fast. Two punches landed before he separated, putting space between us. A thin trickle of blood trailed from his nose. I held my ground, waiting for his next move.

"I'm going to gut you just like your father," Hugo growled.

What the actual hell? "He died in a car accident." Engaging was a mistake, but I couldn't stop myself. I'd had my suspicions that there was more to what had happened to my parents. That he'd killed them wasn't a shock.

We circled each other but held back from striking. I had to know. As soon as he spilled his brand of verbal poison, I would end him.

"Your mom died on impact."

"Shut up." I couldn't... Pain from her loss when I was young sliced my heart. I wanted him to stop talking, dredging up the past.

"Not your dad."

A red haze of fury coated my sight. I lunged, my fist barreling into the side of his face. Hugo's head knocked back. After spitting a mouthful of blood onto the cement, he advanced.

We traded blows, broke apart, then met in a fury of kicks, punches, and martial-arts maneuvers. When I was young, I hadn't stood a chance. There was a point when we would have been evenly matched. Not anymore. I'd learned more. He fought dirty, but so did I.

"Why?" I clipped out between the hit I delivered to his chest. I weaved to the side as he kicked my leg.

"Why what?" Hugo's sick grin taunted me. "Why did I kill my brother and your mother?" He laughed.

I smashed my fist into his face, enjoying the blood that sprayed from his mouth.

He laughed. "Your father wanted out." Hugo evaded my foot. "That couldn't happen. Luckily, you would be his replacement."

"No. They never brought me to Jamal." It had to be a lie. Even as I said it, memories of sparring with my dad in our backyard flooded my mind. *Had he been training me? Was it in case I would need to defend myself if there was trouble, or was he prepping me for initiation into the Dark Wings?*

My vision blurred as he got in a solid hit to my temple. I switched tactics and pummeled his face then gut. When he struck back, I spun out of his way. The urge to destroy him was riding me hard. I held back. I had to hear what he had to say even if it wasn't what I wanted.

Hugo wiped a hand across his left eye, clearing some of the blood. "Your mom got to him, convinced him you could have a different life from what you were born to become, if only he left the mercenary group."

"That's where you came in," I clipped out.

"It is. We couldn't lose the influence, the position we had with the Dark Wings." Hugo's fist slammed into my gut. "Upon your parents' deaths, I owned you. Still do."

I was done. There was nothing more he could say. I unleashed my need to make him pay for everything he'd stripped away from me. My fists hammered into him with relentless speed and force. He staggered back and dropped to one knee. I kept it up. Blood sprayed from his head. He swayed, his face a mass of contusions and swelling.

Five minutes passed, then ten as we exchanged blows. Then I had him on his back, my knife at his throat. My hand shook with the need to sever his carotid artery. He was responsible for my parents' deaths, my stolen childhood, and untold suffering, and I wanted him to die.

Jack brought me back. "We still need answers from him."

He kneeled beside me, his gun pressed against Hugo's temple. Kara's hand rested against my back. Her touch, her support, sent a jolt through me. The awareness her presence brought leashed my blind fury to a manageable degree. It eased the red haze and allowed rational thoughts to return. Hugo couldn't live, but Jack was right. We did need answers.

Hugo chuckled. I pressed the blade of my knife harder against the side of his throat. "Search him." I issued the command to Jack or Kara—it didn't matter. Hugo wasn't going anywhere. He wouldn't leave that parking garage.

Kara's hands were a flurry of motion as she ran them over him, delving into pockets and coming up empty... until she didn't.

Kara opened a small box, flashed the remaining drones, then closed it. "Here, Jack." She handed him the box.

She shifted and caught my gaze. Hugo witnessed the look we shared—he saw death in our eyes.

Jack moved his gun from Hugo's temple and used both hands to open the box. "We got 'em!"

"All of them?" I had to make sure before I made my next move.

"Yes," Jack confirmed with a nod and a look in his eyes that told me I was free to do what I needed to do.

My distraction was enough for Hugo to act. He knocked Jack's gun away and shoved my arm with the blade. I let him. I wanted this. It would have been too easy the other way. My only concern was Kara and my team. But it was he and I, the way it always should have been.

He swept his leg and got me off him. He struggled to his feet, but I was too fast. The sound of rubber-soled shoes pounded the cement as my teammates rushed to help. But I wouldn't need it. Not today or ever again.

Quickly and efficiently, I sliced the side of Hugo's neck then flipped him to the ground. Leaning over him, I planted a knee in his chest and whispered, "You have thirty seconds until you bleed out." I'd severed his carotid artery. "No one here will help you." Hugo's eyes went flat. He wouldn't be able to hurt anyone ever again.

Both Jack and Kara remained quiet. I sensed rather than heard the rest of my team fan around us. "Fifteen seconds." We could have sent him to jail—he would have been convicted. The terrorist act alone would have cost him his freedom, but there was always that chance he could reach us from behind bars. I couldn't risk it. Kara understood. My team would too.

As his heart pumped for the last time, the blood flow from the side of his neck all but stopping, I stood. My teammates met my gaze without judgment. In silence, we left Hugo lying there and headed back to the SUV. Someone called it in. The body would be picked up.

Kara cleared her throat, and all eyes shifted to her. "We have one threat left."

She wasn't wrong. "Ahmed," I said. Something needed to be done. Murmurs echoed in the parking garage as the guys agreed.

"That council..." Kara continued. "Would they put it to a vote if they knew who, in addition to the president, hired Hugo?"

"We have evidence in the form of emails between Hugo and Ahmed on the flash drive," Chris confirmed.

A blinding smile curved her lips. "Then let's make it happen."

I laughed. He would get what was coming to him. The council would see to it.

It was finally over. I wrapped my arms around Kara, grateful for her presence. Her touch reminded me what mattered most—her and Lily.

EPILOGUE

KARA

One Month Later

Sunlight reflected off the ocean. I couldn't believe I was in Maine with Keegan and Lily. The view was as beautiful as Lily's infectious peals of laughter as Samir and David chased her along the shoreline. A brisk wind followed after them, swirling both Lily's and my long hair. I tucked several wayward strands behind my ear as goose bumps danced along my exposed arms.

"Are you cold?" Keegan's baritone sent a pulse of awareness through me, and I nodded.

He wrapped his arms around my waist and pulled me to him so my back rested against his solid chest. My heart swelled at the sight of our daughter before us.

"She's happy." His chin rested on my head. "I talked to Liam this morning."

I couldn't take my eyes off Lily. When we lived in Ahmed's house, she'd been guarded and quiet whenever we ventured past the door to our wing. I wished she'd never seen some of the things she had. "What did you talk to Liam about?"

"Building. Right now, I have a place in California."

I stilled in his arms, afraid to read into what he may or may not be telling me. "That's where you went to live after you escaped the Dark Wings?"

"Mm hm. I have an apartment there. I hadn't planned to move anywhere else, not until you and Lily came here. There's land here for me if I want to do something with it."

I turned in his embrace so I could look into his green eyes. As I shifted, he loosened his hold enough so that we faced each other. My palms rested flat on his chest, and I waited, not daring to breathe.

"I'd like you and Lily to live with me, for us to be a real family."

I blinked back the sudden moisture in my eyes. My throat tightened with emotion. I managed a small nod before resting my forehead against him, struggling to regain control. I'd always loved Keegan. I wanted, burned for him. We'd had a few stolen hours together in his tiny room in a mercenary camp, that night in Washington, DC, and in Maine. He was my dream then and could be my future too.

With Samir settled and officially with the love of his life and living at David's house, we were free to follow our hearts. The divorce would go through eventually. It was a formality, as Samir and I had been married only in name, but we were as true to one another as best friends who'd lived through hell could be. I would always be grateful to him. But I wanted the dream—the guy, the kids, and the home. Not only that, but Keegan's team was an extended family, one that was right there, and we could—

"What's wrong?" Keegan tilted my head so I met his gaze.

I shrugged because there was nothing wrong. Everything was so very right, and that alone scared me.

"Everything's going to be okay, Ankara." He closed the distance between us and brushed his lips over mine.

My eyelids fluttered down, and I lost myself to how he made me feel, how he always had and would. My skin heated. With practiced ease, his skillful mouth parted mine, and I lost myself in the heat and passion he elicited every damn time he touched me.

We stood on a beach beneath the cliffs that held Liam and Liv's farm, but everything faded from my consciousness as he explored my mouth. With a will of their own, my hands roamed over his chest and broad shoulders. Then I buried them in his long hair, which curled in loops around my fingers, its softness only adding to my heightened senses.

An excited squeal penetrated the island we'd created for the two of us through touch. Lily's obvious excitement brought reality back, and I laughed as I felt his lips curve into a smile. With reluctance, we eased apart enough for me to settle against him, my cheek to his chest. His strong hand cupped the back of my head, and I snuggled closer.

"What're you thinking?" The deep rumble of his voice echoed under my palms.

I swallowed back the sudden lump in my throat before answering. "That I couldn't have asked for anything more."

"Mama!" Lily yelled behind me.

"Give us a second, Princess," Keegan said to Lily, his commanding voice gentle. "Then we'll build sandcastles."

The sound of the waves crashing was familiar and soothing. Not only that, but it was beautiful there. Even though the weather was very different than Venezuela, there was no place I would rather have been than anywhere with Keegan and Lily. "What exactly are you saying about the land here?" I had to know without a shadow of a doubt that my daughter and I were wanted in the way I'd hoped.

"It's always been mine, if I wanted it. Liam has acres, and we all purchased more for our business. The space is here for us to build on. Most of my crew lives here, and someday, the rest may follow. You like Liv, Mari, and Stella, right?"

"I do." They'd been so welcoming. The guys too.

"Living here, we'd have a built-in extended family with people who care about us, who we can rely on and trust."

I tightened my arms around his waist. "I want that more than anything."

———

Keegan

I RAN my fingers through Kara's long, dark hair. I could feel her holding back. We were starting over, and I didn't want any secrets between us. "But?"

"I don't want to put them at risk. What if—"

God, I loved that woman. She worried about my crew, my family, the ones who'd proven themselves worthy, with whom I held a bond stronger than blood. "What if nothing. Jamal is dead. You don't owe the Dark Wings, should a new leader rise up. And anyway, they owned me until I was sixteen. I only had a few weeks left before I escaped. My debt to them is paid. One month shy will not be enough for them to come here, and I doubt the new leader would want to take us on, knowing we killed Jamal."

She grinned. "You did make your point well to both Jamal and Hugo."

"Better believe it." Hugo was a bad memory, as was Jamal. Our mission was complete. George Hammond had been proven innocent regarding the true nature and intended use of the six prototype drones that were made in his company's former Venezuelan plant. There were other technicalities he was being held accountable for, but they weren't of concern to us.

None of that mattered to me. Kara and my daughter did. The ring I'd bought late the day before was upstairs in our temporary room in Liam and Liv's home. I had plans to ensure she and Lily were citizens, were mine. That too would happen. For the time being, I wanted to make sure that living there with me was what she wanted too.

There were extenuating circumstances, and I couldn't take anything from her. She was too important to me. If she wanted to wait to live together, to get married, I would. "We could build a house for the three of us, unless you'd rather live on your own for a while. Living under Ahmed's—"

Her fingers rested on my lips, stealing my words. "Shh." A blinding smile curved her lips, and her amber eyes shone with a breathtaking light. "I want that. The house. The life. You..."

Desire exploded at her words, and I crushed her to me, my mouth covering hers. Time lost all meaning again until Lily's shrieks filled the air. I released her lips with a tug on the bottom one with my teeth. My forehead rested on hers. "I'd give you the world. You only have to ask."

"There is one thing."

"Name it."

A small smile curved her swollen lips. "A brother or sister for Lily. Maybe not right away—"

I gave her a squeeze as my heart threatened to explode from happiness. "Yes." Threading her fingers with mine, I tugged her with me as we made our way down the beach to where Lily was chasing her other dad with a handful of sand. Never in a million years would I have thought that mission would have resulted in such a euphoric end.

Lily, a small carbon copy of her mother whose eyes looked just like mine, stopped when we got closer. She flashed a big, toothy grin, and the world made sense. I would have gone through everything in my past again if it meant I could have the two of them.

———

Keegan

Two Months Later

AMBIENT LIGHT CAST a warm glow on the overflowing room, and the smell of the feast before us made my mouth water. The swell of voices ebbed and flowed in the dining room as food was passed from one member of my family to the next. Kara sat next to me at Liv and Liam's table with Lily chatting animatedly to Samir, who was on her other side, along with his boyfriend, David, who was next to him.

Kara's hand rested on my thigh, and I didn't think I could possibly be happier. Once a week, we got together for a family meal with everyone who wasn't out on a mission. It was one of Kara's and my favorite things about living with Liv and Liam. And when our home was finally built in a few more months, we would take a turn hosting, as Jack and Hannah, Hawk and Stella, and Chris and Mari did.

Someday, the rest of the team would move to Maine so we could all be together in one place. Matt and Jo were waiting for the kids to complete high school—the need for stability was important for the kids, and we understood completely. Trev would remain in California for the time being because of Jules's career. Mike, Connor, and Hayden were with us from time to time, and I hoped they would eventually live in Maine permanently.

Kara's hand trembled on my leg, and my attention shot to her. A soft smile curved her lips, and I wanted to pull her close. I wanted her always. Her gaze sparkled, but she shifted in her chair, darting a look around the table. *What is she nervous about?* My spine snapped straight. "What's wrong?"

"Not a thing." Her smile grew. "I have an announcement to make, and I thought it would be good to do with our family present."

What the hell is going on? Talking slowed as they became aware of what Kara had said. Finally, the room was silent, with everyone waiting for her to speak.

Her fingers threaded with mine, and I gripped hers tightly. Whatever was wrong, I would fix it—she was my life, and I would do anything for her. The link we shared was unique, and I felt it flare even brighter between us.

"We're going to have a baby." Her voice was quiet but loud enough for everyone present to hear.

The roar of congratulations and well wishes was deafening, but none of that mattered. *A baby. Holy hell.* I released her hand and wove my fingers through her hair, cupping the sides of her head and pulling her close. With my forehead to hers, I took reassurance as our breaths mingled. "Are you sure? When—"

"I'm two months along. Are you happy?"

"You know I am." I kissed her, and the world faded. My hands trembled as I pulled her to me and held her until a high-pitched sound and tug at my elbow got through to us and we pulled apart, albeit reluctantly.

Lily bounced on her toes, excitement vibrating from her in an abundance of energy only children possessed. "Mama! Daddy said I get a sister?"

I scooped her up so she was between us, and Kara laughed. I was Papa, and Samir was Daddy. It worked for us —Lily had two dads. I could share my little girl with the man who'd done everything he could to keep Lily and Kara safe. I owed Samir more than I could ever repay. We included him and David at every family outing and event. They were always welcome and wanted in our lives.

"Or a brother," Kara corrected. "Are you happy about being a big sister, Lily?"

"Yeah! But I want a sister." Then she hopped off my lap, went back to her seat, and chatted to Samir, asking when he would give her a sister too.

After the sea of congratulations died down, I paused on Liv. She was worrying her bottom lip, her gaze bouncing from Liam to Kara. She'd been ill, and my protective instincts flared. "Liv?"

She pushed out a breath and leaned against Liam, who wrapped his arm around her, concern pulling his features taut. "Are you okay, sweetheart?"

"Yes. More than okay." Again, she glanced at Kara, who gave her a tiny nod then grinned and relaxed against me. "I'm expecting too."

"What?" Liam's reaction was comical. Shock then elation, his Irish accent thickening. "We're having a baby?"

Another round of congratulations erupted from all of us. We would have two infants in the same house, unless our place was ready to move in before they arrived. Either way, I didn't care. The news was welcome. They'd been trying for a long time, and after what Liv had gone through with her first husband, we'd all been afraid she couldn't get pregnant again. It was good news, and we would all make sure she was well cared for.

"What are you thinking?" Kara nudged me.

I pulled her chair closer. "That we should get married soon." I wanted her and Lily with every fiber of my being. Circumstances when we were younger had kept us apart, at least during the daytime, and I was elated at the prospect of a new life together. The legs of my chair scraped as I pushed back from the table. I'd asked her already, and she'd said yes and was wearing the ring I'd given her. But in case she wanted a bigger, more traditional gesture, I would drop to a knee in front of everyone and ask her the right way.

Her hand on my arm stopped me. "Yes. Let's get married next weekend." She got up then sat in my lap, her arms winding around my neck as she pressed close, taking control as she liked to do from time to time. "I don't need pretty words, Keegan. I only need you. I love you."

Goddamn, I adore this woman. What did I ever do to deserve her? "I love you too, Kara." I would give her the world.

THE END

————

To continue reading the Gray Ghost series:
https://amymckinleyauthor.com/gray-ghost-series/

Read a sneak peek of a new series that spins off the novella,
Moonlit Mirage.
https://amymckinleyauthor.com/moonlit-destination-series/

————

Keep up with Amy's releases by joining her newsletter!
http://eepurl.com/dEBqJn

If you enjoyed reading MARKED FOR DEATH as much as I did writing it, I hope you'll consider leaving a review.

ACKNOWLEDGMENTS

This is such a bittersweet moment with the end of Keegan and Kara's story, and most likely the last of the Gray Ghost books. I'm leaving the door open a sliver in case one of the guys demand that I tell their story too. But for now, Hannah has a team to gather, train, and send out on dangerous missions. I hope you'll join me on that journey as well! For a sneak peek, read the novella Moonlit Mirage.

There are so many people to thank for going on this edge of your seat ride as the Gray Ghost team went from troubled teens to the men and women they are today. I couldn't have done this without the support of my family. To my husband and kids who have stood by me every step of the way—thank you! Your support means the world to me.

I cherish all the hours spent at Panera writing with the very gifted author and editor, Taylor Anhalt. Her insight and grammatical skills are invaluable.

My two critique partners, talented authors in their own right, have been with me through the entire series, offering thought provoking comments and ideas that have made the story better. Thank you, Kristin Kisska and Emily Albright, for your friendship, advice, and encouragement.

I look forward to weekly coffee with my friend and beta reader Maryellen Newton. We've set and hit some crazy goals over the years! I can't wait to see what's next.

To the fabulous team at Red Adept editing—Kate B. and Kristina B.—who make the process as the book nears publication seamless and enjoyable. How has it been two years already, Kate? Working with Kate has been a phenomenal experience.

Thank you, T.E. Black Designs, for doing an incredible job on the cover design. I'm already looking forward to working with you on the next set of designs.

Last but certainly not least, a special thank you to all the bloggers—especially Itsy Bitsy Book Bits—and readers who have encouraged and helped me along the way, and who continue to make my dream a reality.

Thank you.

ABOUT THE AUTHOR

Amy McKinley is the romantic suspense thriller author of the Gray Ghost Novels, Moonlit Destination Series, the Five Fates paranormal romance books, and several standalone titles. Her edge-of-your-seat books are filled with surprising twists and just the right amount of heat and danger. She lives in Illinois with her husband, two daughters, two sons, and three mischievous cats.

You can find her at:
www.AmyMcKinley.com

Subscribe to Amy's newsletter for cover reveals, book announcements, and giveaways:
http://eepurl.com/dEBqJn